Baffling
Bagatelles

(Bagatelle: in French or German, a trifle;
musically, a short, unpretentious instrumental composition)

By
Patricia Brine

Macbee Publishing
Edmonton, Alberta
2003

Printed in Canada

Baffling Bagatelles

Patricia Brine
Edmonton, Alberta, 2003

Edited by Judy Johnson

Printed in April 2003 by Imagine Ink

Cover photograph by Charles Brine

National Library of Canada Cataloguing in Publication Data

Brine, Patricia Naomi Kathleen, 1938-
  Baffling bagatelles / Patricia Brine.

 ISBN 0-9687986-3-2

 I. Title.
PS8553.R495B33 2003   C813'.6   C2003-910164-9
PR9199.4.B74B33 2003

Acknowledgements

I give thanks for the continued patience and forbearance
of family and friends.

And

I thank my niece, Dr. Leslie Ellestad,
for some very useful medical information.
I promise not to use it nefariously.

And

I thank Fred and Marion Wolfe, bless them,
for feeding and housing me year after year as I did my research
on southern Arizona and monopolized their pool,
and I thank them for
teaching me to love the desert during my many visits there.

And

I thank all of you who buy the books and actually read them,
thereby feeding my writing habit.

(They might not be so free with their hard-earned dollars
if they realized it only encourages me to
write more books in the series.)

(I won't tell them…and they won't know from this because nobody
reads acknowledgements. Except you.)

Chapter 1

"I just heard about Paul. Why didn't you phone to let me know? The news down here doesn't carry anything about what happens in Canada unless one of our citizens is involved." Anthony Clint began his phone call.

"You'd hardly expect it to be news in Arizona, Anthony. It's more than enough it being news in Edmonton. But I haven't phoned you because I've been in a bit of a state since Paul's death. I haven't even responded to letters of condolence, and that's just not me. I'm not usually a procrastinator. I guess I'm just not coping as well as I ought to," Molly replied.

"Don't flog yourself. Grieving takes time."

"I know, Anthony, but I'm annoyed with myself for not dealing with it better. I don't like to be seen as someone who enjoys wallowing in unhappiness. At the same time I'm madder than hell at everybody and everything," she explained. "I'm not patient with things that don't go right in this world at the best of times, and Paul being a victim of a madman was one big wrong."

"I agree, though I never met him. I felt angry when my partner died, and I still feel that way though it has been over a year since he went. I don't suppose people ever quite get over the death of someone they love," Anthony reflected.

There was a short silence as they both lost themselves in their private thoughts. Then Anthony continued.

"I remember how Graham and I used to laugh at you when you'd get in a tizzy over something one minute and be totally calm the next," he reminisced. "A quick snit, and instant forgiveness. That was our Molly."

"That was normal me. Now I'm depressed and depressing," Molly confessed. "I need to get away from here. Every time I turn around I'm reminded of what happened."

"Have the police found out who killed him?" Anthony asked.

"Yes—and the rat who did it is also dead. Let's not talk about it, Anthony. I promise I'll tell you all the details sometime—just not now," Molly replied. "It's too painful."

"Are you back teaching?"

"I haven't had either the courage or the energy to go back to work, and I don't think I can face returning to the same school this fall."

"Then why don't you take a year's leave and come down to Arizona? The bad memories may haunt you less here, and you may be able to start thinking about the good times you and Paul had instead of dwelling on the lost future." The sympathy in Anthony's voice softened the starkness of his words.

"It would be a relief to leave behind my nightmares. I keep seeing blood everywhere and Paul lying in the front hall of our own house." Molly shuddered. "Your offer of an easy escape may be just what I need. My students are better off with their substitute teacher, who just graduated from university and is energetic, willing, and desperate for a job. Students need to be helped to get excited about learning, as you well know, and I don't feel capable of exciting a cat with a fresh piece of liver. I used to really enjoy the kids, but now I just don't have the energy to meet the challenges."

"It isn't as if you haven't done your bit, Molly. You've taught long enough to leave your mark on many, I'm sure. Now it's time to take a break."

"Perhaps you're right. I was quite content to turn my job over to the eager new recruit for the balance of this school year. I haven't even been back to say good-bye to the kids. I guess I'll have to go and bring home all the materials I've acquired over the years, and clean out a few files for my successor. But not yet."

Anthony, sounding lonely, became persuasive. "If you come down, you can move into my guest wing. It'll be almost like having your own apartment—bedroom, bathroom, and a separate room for your bass and computer. No kitchen, though, so you won't have to cook or clean for yourself. If I remember rightly, those are not your favorite activities. I have someone who comes to clean every week, and I'm still an excellent cook. I'd be delighted to cook for you."

Molly wasn't fat, but she was definitely not slim. However, she'd lost a lot of weight since Paul died, and her usually healthy appetite hadn't returned. She used to refer to herself as Rubenesque, but sometimes—mainly when buying clothes—wished she were Twiggy-esque, like the English model who once incited teenagers to mass anorexia. Up to now, Molly had enjoyed eating and enthusiastically admired good cooks and good food. She was everyone's perfect dinner guest.

Anthony went on, "And don't forget, I have the pool so you can swim your lengths every day—you're still keeping fit aren't you? I'll keep the water warm all winter."

The note in Anthony's voice almost suggested to Molly that he needed her to come more than she needed to get away. Why else would he be trying to tempt her?

"What's up, Anthony?" Molly demanded, always direct, never subtle about things she felt she needed to know. "You sound like you need company. Why now?"

"You're right, Molly," Anthony replied, sounding tired. "I also phoned to talk to you because I need a confidant, and when we were at university, you were the one we could all talk to and depend upon. Frankly, I'm having a hell of a time coping myself, and so much is happening in the music department down here, I'm feeling overwhelmed. It was okay when Graham was around to talk it over with, to put everything in perspective, but now I just come home and talk to the walls."

"I've been talking to a few walls myself these last few months, but only because I've driven all my family and friends away by being sulky and whiney and a general pain."

"It's not only Graham's death, but things seem to be getting worse in the music department," Anthony went on, barely hearing her reply. "I feel as if I'm being closed in upon. I need help making decisions, or someone to confirm my judgment of what I think is going on."

"Are you in danger?" Molly asked.

"No, no, no. I would never ask you to come down and join me if I thought I'd be bringing you into another danger zone," Anthony assured her. "It's just me being indecisive. I need a strong person around to shore up my backbone, and you were always good at that."

By the time they finished their phone call, Molly had promised to go to Arizona for the fall and winter sessions at the university, and think about staying for the whole year. She even asked Anthony to look into what she'd need to do to take some classes and bass lessons and play in an orchestra. The Arizona sun, Anthony's obvious need, and the rainiest summer she had ever remembered in Edmonton all made it easy for her to make the decision to leave the city.

Having promised Anthony she would come, she'd have to keep her word. She had trapped herself. She couldn't renege. She began to call her children to tell them her plans.

* * *

Molly's eldest child, Shannon, answered right away.

"Great," she exclaimed in response to the news of Molly's imminent departure to the sunny south. Not blessed with any more patient a nature than her mother, she'd become exasperated with Molly's passivity over the past several weeks. "Have you started packing yet? When do you leave? How long do you expect to be away from Edmonton?" Shannon asked without giving Molly time to answer.

Shannon, taller and slimmer than her mother, had Molly's dark, naturally curly hair, worn shoulder length in loose waves framing her face. She was an energetic woman who'd been ready to take over the world from the moment she was born. Like her mother, or in spite of her, she became a bass player and was considered fortunate among musicians because she had a regular, paying job with the local symphony orchestra. Most people don't realize how many years of training and how much time and money it takes to become a good musician. And most have no idea of the cost of string instruments and repairs necessary to keep them in good form. Getting through the audition process and acquiring a job is another difficult hurdle. People who want to become career musicians must almost consider it a "calling" in order to survive.

"Maybe one term at the university, or maybe longer. I'm going to take a year's leave. That way I'll be able to play it by ear," Molly answered, then added almost petulantly, "You're not even pretending to be sorry your dear old mother is leaving."

Shannon and her mother were close, in spite of frequent altercations, a result of their insistence on being almost too honest with each other.

"I don't want to sound cruel, dear old mother yourself, but we've all been wondering when you'd stop being so morose. I know four months is a short time, and we all miss Paul and understand why you're not in good shape, but...well, really, you've been too remote and unapproachable since he died, and we've missed you. Anyway, feeling sorry for yourself is not your style."

A remorseful Molly said, "I'm sorry. I know I haven't been good company, but you must try to be a little more tolerant, and I'll try to behave more acceptably."

"Why don't we have dinner together, and you can tell us your plans?" Shannon was on summer break from the symphony, so had time for spur-of-the-moment pursuits. Unlike her mother, she enjoyed cooking.

"I'd like that. I think I'm even feeling hungry."

"You'd better have an appetite. You've lost too much weight," Shannon said, and laughed. "I bet you never thought anyone would say that to you, did you? But you look gaunt, and I don't want to waste my cooking on you if you're only going to peck away at it."

"Don't be bossy, dear," Molly responded automatically. "However, I promise I'll have a good appetite. Let's make it for seven o'clock so your sister and brother can come, too."

Shannon agreed and they finished planning the evening.

After Molly had reached Patrick and Erin, she began setting the table. As she finished, the sun began to filter through the cloud cover. It might be a sunny evening, after all. Perhaps it, too, was celebrating her change of mood.

Molly suddenly realized she was looking forward to leaving the city. She didn't like the dark, long winters and tended to get depressed when the sun rose after most people had gone to school or work and set before they returned home. She could never have taught in one of those schools built when the current vogue was to reduce energy needs and distractions for students by having no windows in the classrooms. She was sure it wasn't good for any human being to live constantly in artificial light. She knew she needed the long summer days to recharge her batteries so she could face the following winter. This summer's clouds and daytime rain had been unusual and oppressive. They made Molly feel cheated.

As she anticipated her departure, Molly wondered what was causing Anthony problems in the music department. She expected he just needed her ear, and she'd have nothing more difficult to do than commiserate with him about ordinary problems. She'd be able to concentrate on keeping up with her class work and practicing. Her mind filled with an idyllic view of the Arizona sun, classes taught by gifted professors, hours of freedom to practice. She would leave her worries behind. There would be nothing in Arizona to remind her of the school she was leaving, colleagues who had been killed. Those memories could be left here in Edmonton, home of what was at one time the largest indoor shopping mall in the world, and the former home of hockey star Wayne Gretzky—the only claims to fame the city had, as far as Molly knew.

* * *

Dinner with the children went well—lots of wine, lots of stories about Paul—a wake of sorts, the kind of party Paul would have liked. The stories made them laugh and shed tears of joy and pain. Cathartic for all, it was particularly appreciated by Molly, who had denied herself this celebration of Paul's life until now.

That night, after everyone had gone home, Molly managed to get the best real sleep she'd had since Paul was murdered. She woke the next morning refreshed and ready for the world.

Chapter 2

"No, Trent, I can't do that." Anthony Clint wasn't enjoying his role as chairman of the music department at Arizona University, and was very glad the appointment would be over at the end of the following year. Then sabbatical, wonderful sabbatical. He looked forward to having time to write, followed by a return to teaching, instead of administration. He'd made a mistake by accepting the position, but at the time thought it would be good for his career. He soon discovered teaching and composing were more to his taste, and career advancement wasn't as important to him as he thought.

Trent Quillium taxed his patience from the very beginning. The lad was a gifted cellist, but unfortunate physically. His gangly arms and legs gave the impression he never had a decent meal, and the blond hair framing his spotty face always looked unwashed and uncombed. Anthony thought the boy needed a good mother or wife to put him together. A less charitable colleague called him "one of God's shop projects."

Trent had adored his composition teacher, Graham Winslow, and had followed him around, hanging on his every word. In his quest for a recipient worthy of his devotion since Graham's death, Trent alienated many members of the music department. Being a talented player and composer wasn't enough to keep him from being shunned. Anthony couldn't bring himself to reject Trent, too, though he shuddered at the thought of being responsible for this boy, who seemed so naive and vulnerable.

Now Trent was demanding that the university plan a memorial for Graham. He seemed to think the memory of Graham should live on in their hearts and minds forever, and was distressed that the entire student body and faculty did not share his intense emotional response to Graham's death.

"It's not asking too much," Trent pleaded. "I just don't see why we can't dedicate the music department's first chamber music concert to his memory. Nothing was done for him last year. The Fauré quartet, one of his favorites, is on the program."

Anthony had already turned down many of what he considered Trent's more excessive proposals. This latest one was the most reasonable, though Anthony still thought it was too long after Graham's death. He didn't like these constant reminders. Maybe if he agreed to a dedication at the chamber music concert, it would fulfill the boy's need and release him from this obsession.

"Have you spoken to any of the members of the quartet about it?"

"Yes, today. They say it's all right with them. They said I just had to clear it with you."

Anthony thought for a moment and then came to a decision. "I'll talk to the members of the quartet at their next rehearsal. If they still find the idea acceptable, I'll check with other members of the department to see what they think. If it seems to have everyone's approval, we'll do it."

Trent's eyes filled with tears. "Oh, thank you, thank you. I'll never forget this. You'll never regret it."

"Don't thank me. It hasn't happened yet. Now, I have a lot of paperwork to wade through, so let me get to it."

"Yes, sir." Trent loped to the door. There he paused and looked back. "The quartet is rehearsing in the orchestra room this afternoon."

A quick smile and he was gone. Something about the smile sparked a memory. Anthony couldn't identify of whom it reminded him, but it was someone he'd once cared about. The tossed remark, the sudden departure. The memory escaped before he could trace it, leaving him vaguely nostalgic.

Anthony sighed. He wished he felt more compassion toward the poor lost boy, but he didn't seem to have the strength these days. He supposed he'd better deal with the memorial immediately. He wished Trent had managed to graduate last year, as he should have. Instead, he had taken a year off for reasons into which Anthony had never looked.

Just as he was getting his mind centered on the everlasting paperwork, Anthony's secretary, Joey, stuck her head in to tell him his nemesis,

Ruby Reddick, wanted to see him. Ruby was one of those people who raised the hair on the back of his neck. He never really knew what she was up to. When she was in his office, he kept the door to Joey's area open wide. It was always bad news when Ruby came.

"Why didn't I get the money?" she asked belligerently, firing the first salvo.

"To what are you referring?" Anthony asked, determined to be patient, polite, and careful.

"Scholarship money, of course. I'm an excellent student, my marks are high, and I am a very good musician. I deserve scholarship money," she explained, in a tone of voice usually reserved for chastising a child.

"I'm afraid I can't help you with that," Anthony replied. "We have a duly appointed scholarship committee assigned to make all those choices. The decisions as to who will receive the money are based on marks, performance, involvement in the musical affairs of the university, need, and, finally, the interview."

"You were on that committee. So, tell me who voted against me and why," Ruby insisted, her voice rising in anger.

"Any queries should be made in writing and addressed to the committee," Anthony forged ahead. "I am not at liberty to divulge the committee's thoughts as they deliberated. I can only assure you they were fair and considerate."

"Bullshit," Ruby exploded. "The recipients are all your little favorites. Your toadies. You're going to be sorry you made those decisions," she yelled, and strode out of the office.

Joey came to the door after Ruby left. "I can see why you leave the door open. Is she going to make trouble?"

"I hope not, Joey, but with Ruby it's hard to tell. She's always been devious and temperamental. Her interview revealed that, and it was part of the reason the committee chose other equally capable students over her. Obviously, she doesn't understand her attitude is against her. I'm not sure how she gets the 'favorites' bit, either." Anthony shuffled some papers on his desk. "Oh, well, I expect we'll find out before we want to."

He sighed like a falling soufflé and picked up his pen to get at his paperwork.

* * *

That evening when he got home, Anthony phoned Molly.

"I'm calling to make sure you haven't changed your mind," he began, sounding depressed. "I just got in. This chairman job is a colossal pain. I'm sick of it all...the complaints, troublemaking students, trying to find money for scholarships and honorary chairs...socializing...committee meetings...budgets. It never stops. The only thing that kept me going today was the hope I'd have someone to cook for soon. Is it really true? You are coming? I didn't dream it?"

"Yes, I'm coming, Anthony," she assured him. "I haven't decided what day I'm leaving yet, but I'll be driving down before the end of August. I want to arrive well before classes start. Have you found out what I need to do to register as a special student? I don't feel like working on a degree, but I'd like to take some classes in music history, and some bass lessons. And I really want to play in an orchestra while I'm there. You know I've never been good at sitting around twiddling my thumbs."

Anthony and Molly discussed the many preparations to be made and details to be looked after before she could be accepted as a student. There wasn't much time, and she was glad Anthony, as chairman of the music department (she'd always refused to call him "the chair," insisting, in her own obstinate way, he was a man and not a chair) could look after most of the arrangements for her.

"Do you know if Helene Hanson is studying there, Anthony? She's a viola player who came down last year."

"Yes. I see her around quite a bit. She's one of our graduate students and plays in the orchestra as well. A good musician."

"She is. She used to play in one of the orchestras here with me, and is a friend of mine, but we've lost touch since she got married and moved to Tucson. We used to teach together, too. But she's not a letter writer, and she's not into computers, so no e-mail, either. Anyway, if you see her before I come down, would you tell her I'm coming? I know I won't have time to see her before classes start, but I'd like to be in touch with her as soon as I'm settled in. It'll be nice to have another friend there."

"I'll do what I can, Molly," Anthony said, "but I can't promise anything. I'm a little overwhelmed at the moment with an increasing number of small problems—all of which seem to require my instant attention."

"That sounds heavy, Anthony," Molly responded. "Don't worry about Helene for now, then. I'll get her number from you when I come down. Is there anything I can do to make things easier for you before I get there?"

"Nothing I can think of, Molly," Anthony replied. "Unless you can tell me why my department seems to have more than its share of odd faculty, and students who seem determined to drive me mad. Come down quickly and bring sanity into my life."

"It couldn't be that bad, surely," Molly said with apprehension. She wanted peace in her life right now.

"You will make it better. I'm looking forward to your arrival," Anthony assured her.

* * *

After spending the next morning running errands, Molly arrived home to see the light on her answering machine blinking. The first message was from Anthony. Her heart sank as she listened.

"I know you're going to hate this, Molly, but you must audition to get into the bass instructor's studio and the orchestra. Even though the registrar of the university is a friend of mine, we can't do everything. The bass teacher here is a decent person, a gentle soul, and a very good teacher. But he still insists on an audition. Call me at my office number any time up to four o'clock so we can plan for it."

Auditions.

Auditions always terrified her. Even thinking about them brought back memories of past horrors, and her finger trembled as she pushed the numbers for Anthony's office phone.

"I can't do it, Anthony," she said when he answered. "I've never been able to audition, and I can't think of any reason why things would have changed. I just completely fall apart. Do you think the bass teacher would give me a chance if I explained I don't expect to become a great bass player…just a better teacher?"

"I don't think so, Molly. He wants to hear you, not exclude you, just so he has an idea of what he's getting. What about using a beta blocker? Shannon used one when she was auditioning, didn't she?" Anthony remembered Molly's eldest daughter's fears about having to prove herself at a fifteen-minute audition after studying for almost a lifetime, knowing what an attack of nerves could do to your bow arm and, ultimately, your professional chances.

"That's true. She had to go to the doctor for a checkup and get a prescription for it, though. It's a little dangerous because it apparently works by lowering the blood pressure. Shannon had to experiment with it first to figure out how much she needed to keep her nerves calm enough for her recitals and auditions. I just never thought of the beta blocker as being something for me, because I don't do auditions for jobs, and I'm certainly never going to be giving a recital. I worry about taking drugs."

"Don't be so silly, Molly. Some drugs are good when taken properly and for the right reasons. All this stuff does is reduce the physical side effects of nervousness. Many professional musicians resort to beta blockers for recitals or concerts as well as auditions. Then they're free to concentrate on doing what they're good at, not on whether they can stop their hand or bow from shaking. I've heard a lot of heart and brain surgeons use them, too."

Molly never pretended to be a great bass player, though some friends who had no musical background or training thought she was. Students and their parents who heard her play, and knew she had once played professionally, thought her an accomplished musician; however, compared to the talented and well trained bassists she heard at every International Society of Bassists' convention she took her students to, she would be considered a hack at worst or a poseur at best.

"Are you still there, Molly?" Anthony Clint complained. "You've always been such a twit about medication."

"Oh, Anthony, don't chide me. I don't have much patience with these things. Just make an appointment for me to take the audition as late as possible in August, and I'll get busy practicing. I haven't played the bass since Paul's death, and my muscles are like jelly. And, yes, I'll make an appointment with the doctor to see about the beta blocker."

"I understand. But come down, and you'll be so busy you won't have time to feel sorry for yourself. I've faxed all the papers you need to sign and submit, and listed what you need to send, so don't forget to check your machine. There's room in the contemporary music history class for you, and don't worry too much about orchestra. They're very short of bassists this year, so you'll probably get in."

"Thanks a lot, Anthony." She laughed at his efforts to set her at ease with a comment most musicians would consider a grave insult. "That will really inspire me."

"I just wanted to make sure you knew you're needed and likely to get in without any trouble in case you heard anything about the conductor. He's a fine musician, but a nasty man when he's not exercising his charm, which is considerable. I don't mean to scare you off, as he does have good credentials, but I've had a few complaints about him."

"I can usually tolerate most conductors as long as they don't talk too much—it's so boring sitting there snoozing off while some of them go on and on. Most musicians dislike most conductors, anyway. They're rarely spoken of with great love or, in some cases, even respect. There seem to be a lot of them who are either good musicians or good people, but not many are both," Molly said. "It takes a lot of ego to have the confidence to be a conductor, so I feel a little sympathy for them. Don't worry, Anthony. I'll be okay. If I don't make it into the lessons or orchestra, I'll just come home again."

"I don't want you to do that," Anthony said, sounding stricken.

"I'll practice very hard," Molly assured him, and they rang off.

Molly was a little daunted by what she'd agreed to do. Auditions in not much more than a month. Gulp. Oh, well, if she didn't make it, at least it wasn't life threatening. She phoned Shannon to tell her about the audition.

"Since you are now the family professional, our resident performer on the kontrabass, string bass, double bass, or whatever you call your instrument these days," Molly concluded, "I wonder if you could pop over today and help me choose pieces and symphony excerpts to work on, and give me advice."

"I'm calling it a bass, Mom, as you well know, especially during my summer break. It's only when I'm tired and it feels heavy that I call it anything else. But you asking me for help—this is like the mountain coming to Mohammed," Shannon replied. "After all the students you've prepared for auditions, you're asking ME to prepare YOU? Here I always thought you were the Ann Landers of the bass world."

"Hardly. The mother has now become the child. Don't whine at me. Just help me. I am panic stricken already over the thought of doing this. Need I remind you I fall apart at auditions? Always have, likely always will."

"Mom, you don't need me. Just teach yourself." Shannon sounded exasperated.

"You mean, take my own advice?" Molly said mockingly. "That's a novel idea."

"You've taught a million kids after seducing the poor things into the bass world with your crazed enthusiasm. Think of all the parents who have been trapped into driving their kids and their basses around. And your own kid who you dragged, kicking and screaming, into learning the bass, too. Now it's your turn."

"It was cheaper than paying for lessons elsewhere, and you're not kicking and screaming now."

"Right. I'm hooked. What's more, even employed, oh rapture. But getting back to you, just practice what you preached as you prepared us for our recitals...auditions...festivals...exams."

"It's different when it's for me. I was just giving kids performance stars to shoot for, and deadlines, so they'd practice and become good enough to enjoy their music. Just building audiences for the kind of concerts you play. Remember, I'm what pompous musicians talk about when they say, 'Some people can do, others teach.'"

"Don't be an ass, Mom. If teachers spent the time practicing their instruments instead of working with their students, they'd probably be better players. You chose teaching instead of performing. It takes determination and dedication for both."

"I'm pretty determined, but not very disciplined, I'm afraid. There are always too many other things to do."

"But you're usually energetic—some would say 'driven.' So, drive yourself." Then Shannon relented. "Okay, I'll be your guru for the next month. By the time I come over later this afternoon, I expect you to have warmed up with the scale cycle and some bowing exercises. We'll choose some music for you to prepare, and I'll assign you some goals."

"I feel driven already. I'll pretend I'm preparing for a workshop with Gary Karr or Jeff Bradetich."

"Or John Clayton or David Young—any one of them will do. As you practice, think of all their advice from those big 'bass love-in' workshops we had. Imagine the kind of sound they made, and then make that your goal. Just like you always told us." Shannon's voice took on a nostalgic tone. "Remember how Gary Karr always made us feel we were 'the chosen' because we played bass? We always practiced so hard after his workshops, trying to live up to the image."

"He's such a sweetie. But when I listen to him play, I wonder why I've ever dared pretend to be able to play at all," Molly said, taking up the praise of one of their favorite solo bass performers. "I wish we'd hear more bass soloists like Gary Karr on the concert circuit. Their playing is on a par with that of Yehudi Menuhin and Yo Yo Ma, but they don't get as many gigs. I must speak to your artistic director about it again. I get so tired of all the attention given to solo violinists, cellists, and pianists. Do you suppose they're hired more often because they're a dime a dozen and easier and cheaper to get?"

"Don't call them a dime a dozen around your violin and piano playing friends. You may not survive the encounter. Try 'plentiful' instead," Shannon warned. "Actually, they're probably hired because most people are more familiar with those instruments, so ticket sales will be better…and they're definitely not cheaper."

"I suppose," Molly admitted reluctantly, "and I'll take your warning. Some violinists are so irritating, though. Especially first violinists. They seem to think they're the only musicians in an orchestra and the rest of us are there just to serve them. They get quite annoyed with me when I tell them they're just playing small basses." Molly smiled as she said it.

"This chitchat is all very nice, Mom, but it's only postponing your practice time. Get going."

"Yes, ma'am. See you later, dear," Molly replied, pretending to be cowed.

Shannon said sternly, "Don't think I'm taken in by that tone of voice, either. I'm looking for results, not words."

Molly recognized the tone of voice. It was the one she'd used when dealing with Shannon in her adolescent years.

* * *

Jolene, flushed and exhausted, put her violin lovingly into the case after wrapping it carefully in its protective cloth. Four hours. She'd done more today than she could ever hope for. But she'd better get the instrument, the music, and the stand put away before he got back.

She was already tired by the time her husband left for work this morning. She almost gave up and went back to bed instead of practicing. She'd expended too much energy on their argument, and then wasted another hour thinking of things she should have said and done, before she came to her senses and realized she was just playing into his hands. He'd debilitated her again.

But not quite. She'd rallied.

The great conductor, Lance Sneazewell. He was such a bastard. She should just leave him, but she knew what he was like, and what he did to people who tried to cross him. She'd already ruined her chances for a decent career by marrying him, anyway.

But he didn't know her secret. Every time he was out, she practiced and practiced. He wouldn't tolerate her practicing when he was home. That was one way of keeping her down, in addition to the disparaging remarks intended to convince her she would never be good enough for the audition circuit. He didn't want her to be capable. But she was determined not to be squelched. By the time she decided how she was going to get away from him, she would be playing brilliantly again.

He was so powerful, though. She didn't know how he managed to manipulate people. Maybe he charmed others the way he had charmed her when they first met, she thought bitterly. If she left him, he might ruin her audition chances, tell people she was incompetent. He could be so persuasive if it suited him. She'd seen him operate.

But for those over whom he had power, he had no kind words, no charm, and no sympathy.

* * *

Trent wasn't sure he could survive much longer. The world was so cold and unfriendly. He wasn't even able to compose anything anymore. He wasn't practicing his cello—he just didn't have the drive. It was going to be impossible to tolerate his classes and that vicious orchestra conductor for the whole year. But if he didn't, that would be the end of everything for him. And if that was the case, he would make it final this time.

His first mentor, Graham Winslow, had been such a kind man. But now he was dead. Everyone was dying around him except the people who didn't deserve to live. There was nobody left who cared about him and, except for Anthony, no one he cared about. And now Anthony barely acknowledged his existence.

Trent decided to try once more to get through to someone—to reach anyone. He needed someone who would understand his pain…or help him feel part of the world again. Today he would make his last effort.

I'll go to Anthony, he thought. If he doesn't listen, that's the end.

Chapter 3

"Why are you driving all that way?" Ann O'Connor asked her daughter when Molly phoned the Peace River contingent of her family to tell them her plans.

"I'll need both a car and my bass there. It's the only way. It'll take only three days at the most and, yes, I'll drive carefully. Want to come with me?"

"If I were younger, I would. Now I fly," Ann replied. There was a momentary pause. "On the other hand, at my age I'm not in a rush to get anywhere, and if I come with you, it will make you stop each day before you get too tired to drive carefully."

"Can I take back my invitation?" Molly asked, teasing her mother, whose company she generally enjoyed and with whom she traveled well.

"No. I'm coming. I'll fly down to Edmonton a few days before you leave so I can visit with your sister. Is the granny annex available?"

"There are no other grannies dropping by to use it. We're fresh out of grannies in residence."

"Good. I'll phone to let you know what plane I'm on," she said, ignoring Molly's attempt at a joke, and hung up.

Molly phoned Anthony right away to let him know he would have an extra guest and to warn him about her mother's insistence on being an active participant in whatever was going on. She suspected Anthony would enjoy Ann, but not without some warning of her impending arrival.

***

"I am placing you at the back of the second violin section," Lance told his wife as he undressed for bed. "I don't want your prima donna hysterics about it, either. It's time you learned what it's like to pull your own weight in an orchestra, instead of swanning your way through solos as if you were the next Heifetz." He snorted with disgust as he looked down his aristocratic nose at her. "Don't you wish. You're lucky I consider you good enough to play in my orchestra at all, so don't start getting uppity again, demanding to be put in the first violin section. And don't turn your snotty little nose up, either."

Jolene eyed him with loathing as he left the room to brush his teeth.

"And make sure you're up in time to get my breakfast in the morning," he continued to harangue her as he returned from the bathroom. "You're getting a little lazy. I'm earning the money. Your job is to look after me. See that the food is on the table by eight. You're not much good for anything, but you could try."

Jolene kept her mouth shut. Silence was the safest reaction, especially now. She didn't want to warn him of her plans. She was not going to take his crap much longer. If she let herself go now, it would spoil everything. She wasn't in a hurry and wasn't like his former wives. She was in control—only he didn't know it yet.

Jolene wondered how she could have thought Dr. Lance Sneazewell was such a charmer. She simulated a slight snore, though she knew it wouldn't discourage Lance. If he wasn't finished with her, he'd just wake her up. Other people didn't have feelings or needs as far as he was concerned. They existed to serve him. What a fool she'd been not to see what he was from the beginning. But she couldn't admit to Daddy that he'd been right when he told her she shouldn't marry this man.

* * *

"Georgia, I'd like to talk to you," Helene began, having skipped her orchestra rehearsal so she could get home before Edwin and have some time alone with her daughter. She knew Georgia was in her bedroom because she'd heard the sound of the door being locked when she walked down the hall. "Please open up."

"What do you want?" Georgia opened the door so quickly, it seemed she must have been standing just next to it, her beautiful face marred by a sullen expression. Helene, incongruously, was suddenly re-minded of haughty models glaring out at the general public from the pages of glamour magazines at the supermarket. Her heart tightened, and she found it hard to breathe. What do I say now? she wondered. Her tongue seemed incapable of moving, and she wished her eyes could do all the talking. But as Helene reached out to hug her daughter, Georgia shrank back.

"What do you want?" she practically snarled at Helene.

Helene let her arms drop and her resolve falter. How could she ask what was wrong without it seeming like a confrontation? Did Georgia mean for her rejection to hurt? And why? She steeled herself to go on trying.

"What's wrong? What's happening with you? How can I help?" Helene asked all in one breath not wanting to lose Georgia's attention. Her daughter's expression began to change, her eyes filling with tears.

At that moment, the door banged open and Edwin came into the house, his arms filled with grocery bags. Helene turned to look at him.

"I'm home," he announced in a happy voice. When he saw Helene, his look changed to one of surprise. Or was it dismay? "I thought you had orchestra tonight. You're home early."

Helene was too stunned to speak. Didn't he have late office hours on Tuesdays? She'd wanted to have time alone with her daughter. She turned back to Georgia just as the door to the bedroom closed again. She heard the click as the lock was turned into place.

"I got all the things you said you wanted from the store." Edwin motioned with the bags and went to the kitchen.

Helene tried to respond pleasantly. Edwin did all the shopping for the family, and she did appreciate his help. But all she could think of was her moment with Georgia, now lost. She was determined to make sure they had another chance very soon.

* * *

When Molly and Ann finally got away from Edmonton in mid-August, the first day of travel was almost relaxing. Molly had been so busy getting organized for the trip and preparing for her audition, she was totally exhausted. It was a relief not to be able to do anything but drive. She'd borrowed a large variety of book tapes from the library, planning to send them back to Edmonton with Ann, who would be staying in Arizona for only a few weeks.

"What would you like to listen to first?" Molly asked Ann after they had passed Red Deer, the small city about halfway to Calgary, three hours south of Edmonton. They were enjoying the rolling farmland and beautiful farm buildings they passed along the way.

"Something pleasant, dear," Ann had replied. "None of those gory murder books or terribly earnest prize-winning books you feel obligated to listen to, thinking you can pretend you've read them."

"I don't listen to them just to 'pretend' I've read them, Mother," Molly replied with annoyance. "I read for entertainment, and I find most of the prize-winners highly depressing rather than entertaining. They tend to be peopled with characters who are a psychological mess and blame their warped personalities on their horrid mothers—hmm...now why didn't I think of such a ploy?" she mused. "Maybe I should try to use my upbringing as an excuse for my problems."

"Give me an example. I don't remember you being anything but spoiled rotten," Ann demanded.

"Oh, all right, I made it up. I can't remember any specific instances, either. But the prize-winning books do leave me with the impression the authors are whining about their families or they don't much like their parents, particularly their mothers—we have an inordinately strong influence on our offspring, wouldn't you think? I sometimes wonder if being depressing is a prerequisite for winning a prize. I can never think of the specific writings or authors because I put them out of my mind as soon as I finish their books. I'm tired of reading about the horrible lives of people sunk in situations where nothing ever seems to improve—like the mother in *Angela's Ashes* who puts up with crap from her husband, year after year after year, ad nauseam. I want to scream at her to do something about it—like get fixed, or get rid of the man. I don't have sympathy with people who remain in relationships with people who are just destroying them or their children."

"You don't understand about people getting trapped in situations, Molly. These books are just trying to tell you there are people who are different from you, who can't get themselves out of these difficulties."

"I will never understand, no matter how many books are written about them. I'd make a lousy counselor, wouldn't I?"

"I agree, dear. So, why do you listen to these books on tape if you don't find them entertaining?"

"I want to know what the literary types think a good book is. I know I will never be one of the intelligentsia, or enjoy the type of book they revere, but I want to see what's currently 'in,'" Molly replied. "Listening to these writers on book tapes is the easiest way for me to wade through them."

"You enjoyed *The Shipping News*, by that Proulx woman, and it was an award winner," Ann pointed out, both of them having read the book during a long plane ride home from England. "You mustn't go about making sweeping generalizations, Molly."

"Yes, Mommy dearest," Molly replied, making reference to another book they had both read in which the daughter of Joan Crawford told the world what a rotten, abusive mother she'd had. "And I may accidentally find I enjoy another one someday."

"And I resent being called 'Mommy dearest,' Molly. You forget you loaned me the book, or you wouldn't refer to your poor defenseless old mother in such a nasty way," Ann said, not losing a beat in her rhythmic knitting of yet another afghan for her grandchildren, completely unthreatened by the insulting reference.

Molly laughed. Her mother was about as defenseless as a porcupine, happy and secure in the knowledge her son and daughters adored her, in spite of her continued insistence on treating them like recalcitrant children, though they were all over fifty.

"I do want to know what the literati think are good books, though, Mom. Someday I might agree with them. Who knows?"

"Oh, I doubt you'd ever agree, Molly. If something's 'in' you generally think it's not to your liking on principle. Perhaps if the prize-winners go out of favor later, you'll decide they're readable." Ann closed the subject by choosing a tape herself and clicking it into the tape deck.

"This one is a Margaret Taylor Bradford. You must have heard your sister recommending her as an author I would enjoy," Ann said.

Molly groaned, gritted her teeth, and settled in to tolerate her mother's choice. The authors recommended by her eldest sister were not ones Molly generally enjoyed, and she'd had a taste of this author. One taste was quite enough, but she'd chosen it because she knew her sister was right. Her mother would enjoy it.

The scenery on the drive through southern Alberta was more attractive than either of the women had remembered, the mountains dramatic as they peeked over the horizon of the treeless prairie, the valleys looking like inverted mountains.

When they reached the border to the United States, Molly stopped to buy gas and grabbed a Dick Francis from the bag of tapes, quickly loading it into the tape deck. Ann seemed satisfied with the choice.

The border crossing into the United States was no trouble. Molly presented her study documents, Ann her ticket for the airline proving

her intention to return home to Edmonton, and both showed their pass-
ports. As they passed through the Montana plains, the buttes (mesas)
jutting out all along the route made the Great Falls–Helena portion of the
trip well worth the drive. During the course of the day, they worked their
way through a tape of a depressing book by an internationally known
prize-winning author and a generic Harlequin-esque intrigue by Lesley
Grant-Adams before stopping for the night, having driven many more
kilometers than Molly expected or Ann intended.

"Here's a good place to stay, Mom. Cheap and close to the freeway."

"I do not intend to spend the last few years before I drop off staying
in cheap motels for which the only advantage is their close proximity to
the freeway. We will stay over there," Ann said, pointing to a sign directing
them to a more expensive chain of motels. "It is not much further from
the freeway, and more to my taste."

"All right, Mother, but I don't want to spend hours over a meal, so
I insist on a fast service place close by," Molly replied, knowing she
really had no choice but to let her mother have her way. After the long
drive she'd endured, Ann had earned her night's rest in a comfortable
bed. Molly hoped she'd be as durable as her mother when she was
nearly eighty.

"After eating rabbit food and crackers all day, although the carrot
sticks and apples were good, I have earned a decent meal, Molly," Ann
insisted as they drove into the motel parking lot. "I'm feeling quite peckish
and insist on a restaurant with chairs and table service."

Molly demurred. After they'd registered and she'd taken the double
bass to the room, not wanting to leave it unprotected in the car for a
moment, they drove to a nearby family restaurant in keeping with
Ann's requirements.

Ann looked carefully around the dining room as they waited for
their orders to be served.

"Surely those gentlemen know better than to wear their caps while
eating," Ann said in her most carrying voice. "And baseball caps. How
common." Ann almost sniffed, but that would have been in bad taste.

"I guess they didn't have you to bring them up, Mom."

Ann ignored her, still totally immersed in the effrontery of customers
who dared to follow their own path rather than Ann's set of rules.

"They're even chewing with their mouths wide open," she
continued in a shocked voice. She dragged her attention away from
the men and said, "Molly, we must not eat in a place like this

again. I don't wish to be put off my food by the clientele's lack of good manners."

"Sometimes you can be quite embarrassing, Mother," Molly said. "And that is in bad taste, too." She then quickly, but deftly, changed the subject. Soon they were in a discussion of the taped stories they'd listened to in the car. They proceeded to a heated argument about which ones they'd choose for the next day.

When their meals were served, Molly forbore to point out that Ann's appetite didn't seem to be in any way impaired as she tucked into her food. She ate using the best of manners, of course.

* * *

After loading the bass and themselves into the car and driving away from their motel next morning, Ann looked around her and commented, "Helena is much prettier than I had imagined. I love this large valley and the ethereal-looking mountains peering out of the mist." She pointed at the hills. "Look at the wild junipers growing everywhere."

"Goodness, Mom, you sound almost poetic," Molly replied.

Ann smiled beatifically and continued to enjoy the scenery for several miles before putting on the book tape, *The Horse Whisperer*, they'd agreed on at dinner the night before.

The tape was finished by the time they reached Mt. Zion National Park. They were so taken with the sight of the sandstone mountains eroded into fascinating patterns and shapes, they could do nothing but gawk.

When they emerged from the park, Ann said, "I didn't like the last part of *The Horse Whisperer*. Why did the author have to cheapen it with the bit about the woman having an affair with the man who was doing so much good for her family, especially the child? What did it have to do with the wonderful work he was doing with the animals, anyway? These modern novels seem to find it necessary to add sex for the people who look for titillation in the books they read. I suppose it sells books, but it's quite tiresome, and in such bad taste."

"The books and authors of your heyday included sex and love and mushy stuff, too," Molly reminded her.

"But they had the good taste to be discreet, not to be so graphic. They allow your imagination to make it more romantic than a romp in the hay," Ann replied. "At least Dick Francis confines himself to the story rather than adding a bunch of unnecessary sex scenes."

"How about another tape? I have a Ken Follett. It should satisfy you," Molly said mischievously, knowing her mother would be shocked by some of the detailed sex scenes, but would become immersed in the story nevertheless.

"I'm sure it will do nicely," Ann said happily, unaware of its true nature, and looked through the bag of tapes for it.

A few hours later, at Molly's insistence, they took the detour off the main highway to go to the Grand Canyon.

"I suppose I should see it now before I join your father underground. I may not have time left to come this way again," Ann said after having expressed annoyance that Molly was making the drive longer by adding the canyon drive.

As they approached the rim at the village, a deluge of rain obscured their view. Just before they were ready to give up and leave the park, it cleared, so they were able to get out of the car and walk to the rails for a good look.

At the edge of the first overlook, they were glad to see firmly embedded fences strategically placed to prevent the visitors from accidentally popping over the edge. Ann stepped back as though she had been struck the moment she saw the full depth of the canyon, and Molly's stomach lurched as it always did when she looked down on anything from a great height.

"What must they have thought when this was first discovered?" Ann wondered when she'd caught her breath and made her way tentatively back to the restraining rail.

"I don't know, but it frightens me every time I see it. I wonder if the original discoverers emerged from the trees on their horses at full gallop and…whoops…over the edge. Do you see how, in many places, the trees grow right up to the edge? It would be easy to miss the fact there is a dangerous canyon here. Unless the horse was smarter than the human," Molly said.

"Horse and rider over the edge is a gruesome thought. Don't suggest things like that," Ann replied, and continued along the walkway to get a different view. They stopped at a few more viewpoints before the clouds gathered again and a light drizzle, sufficient to send them hurrying back to the car, became a downpour.

"Surely the weather could take pity on an old lady and let her see this in comfort," Ann grumbled as she put on her seat belt.

"Rapid changes of weather are apparently normal for this area, Mom, so the rain wasn't sent just to aggravate you. Sorry," Molly said, laughing. "I'm sure you are surprised and disappointed your comfort and welfare are not the only things on the Creator's mind."

"You are indulging in entirely too much levity at my expense, dear," Ann chastised her daughter good naturedly. "You're not supposed to make fun of your dear old mother. A little more genteel respect would be appreciated."

As they continued their drive, the supply of fat-free sunflower-seed pretzels and apples was sufficient to fend off their hunger pangs. The water bottle they'd filled before they left their motel room quenched their thirst until they reached Flagstaff, where they settled into a mid-price motel for the night after enjoying dinner at a restaurant where even Ann found nothing to complain about.

As Molly had known she would, in spite of the slightly salacious parts, Ann had enjoyed the Ken Follett tape, which finished just before they arrived at Flagstaff. Her only comment about the content was, "I'm surprised you would think of exposing your aging female parent to such as this."

As they settled down for the night, Molly began getting excited about arriving at Anthony's the next day.

"I'm really looking forward to getting in touch with Helene again," she said to Ann. "Although we didn't see a lot of each other, I've missed her. I hope we have more time to visit while I'm down here than we did in Canada."

"You'll be busy like you usually are," Ann replied.

"Well, I must start making more time for friends," Molly said. "We were all miffed with Helene because she rushed off and married this Edwin Hanson, a visiting professor in Edmonton when she was taking a night class at the university. They moved to Tucson as soon as school was out. We never met her husband and didn't even realize she'd married him until she put in her application for a leave and took off."

"Maybe she was afraid you wouldn't approve and decided not to put it to the test, dear," said Ann.

"I wouldn't have approved. It was too quick. Maybe she was right to keep it a secret. I probably would have tried to get her to hold off."

"She can tell you all about him when you get there, dear," Ann said, reaching up to turn off her bedside lamp. "Goodnight. Don't stay awake reading too long."

Molly smiled at Ann, still mothering though Molly was over half a century old herself.

* * *

The third and last day of their trip was relatively short, but Molly felt sorry for her mother, who had put up with the previous long days of travel, so she agreed to a Rosamunde Pilcher tape. Ann listened to it as they drove along the highway through the tree-covered mountains, enjoying the proliferation of cacti on the hills from Flagstaff to Phoenix, where they encountered more rain.

"I thought this was a desert where no rain is expected," Ann commented.

"I thought the August monsoon would be over. Maybe it's just a little late this year," Molly replied. "The landscape is amazingly green. Let's just be glad we're getting to see the results of the rains."

When Molly got out of the air-conditioned car to fill up with gas in Phoenix, she was met with a blast of hot air. The cashier told her it was 108 degrees Fahrenheit in the shade. Neither she nor Ann tried to convert it to Celsius as younger Canadians raised in the metric system would have done. They suffered from having Fahrenheit brains in the Canadian Celsius world. The American imperial system was a welcome change.

South of Tucson, Molly noticed the mileage was signed in metric units.

"Remind me to ask Anthony why when we get there," she instructed Ann, not realizing her mother had been lulled to sleep by Rosamunde Pilcher. She slept on, and woke with a start when Molly stopped the car in the driveway of Anthony's home.

Anthony, looking like an amiable teddy bear with his bushy mustache and beard, came trotting out of the house to greet them and practically squished them with his big, welcoming hugs. He led Ann into the air-conditioned house, suggesting "the lovely lady shouldn't have to put up with this heat while we get the bags out of the car," and returned to help Molly unpack everything before the heat became too much for them. He left her to carry her bass, knowing musicians prefer to carry their own precious instruments, no matter how heavy. It took several trips to take in all their bags and Molly's gear for the year. By the time they were done, Ann looked a little less wilted, and the aroma of the dinner Anthony had already prepared seemed to fill her with happy anticipation.

Ann was captivated by the house, the food, and the service. Anthony plied her with a glass of good wine before sitting her down to a finely set table that met her rigorous standards. Dinner was one of Anthony's best culinary efforts.

When Molly had cleaned her plate, she wiped her mouth on her serviette and leaned back in her chair. "My compliments to the chef, Anthony."

"And not even too spicy," Ann added. "Do you eat like this every night?"

"I will while you beautiful ladies are here," Anthony said, bowing his head in Ann's direction. "I love to cook for people who enjoy eating."

Ann preened herself and smiled happily. She was well fed, well drunk, and well mellowed. She soon began to look tired.

"I'm ready to sleep for a week," she said, admitting, for the first time, how trying the long drive had been for her.

"But you won't, of course," Molly said. "You'd be too afraid of missing something."

"Not tonight," Ann assured her, allowing herself to be ushered out of the kitchen and down the hall to her bedroom. She was soon fast asleep in the comfortable bed Anthony had even left turned down for her.

As they cleaned up the dishes, Molly remembered the question she'd intended to ask Anthony. "Why do the road signs just south of Tucson and all the way here to Green Valley give the distance in kilometers instead of the usual miles? And why do they still mark the speed in miles per hour instead of kilometers per hour to match?"

"The government was trying out the metric system a while back, and this road was a good place to experiment because it ends at the Mexican border and Mexico is metric, of course. They didn't change the speed to kilometers, though, because they thought people would take it as miles per hour and end up speeding. The experiment was ultimately abandoned except for this stretch of the highway. I know not why, but who can ever understand the weird workings of the government?" Anthony replied.

* * *

After they'd finished clearing up, Molly phoned Shannon.

"Has your bass dried out yet?" Shannon asked, always concerned for the instrument.

"I haven't heard it crying from the dryness of the place, but we just arrived. Remember, the province of Alberta is considered to be as dry as the desert—nearly as dry as it is here. In the winter, anyway. A northern desert, so to speak."

"You'd better buy a humidifier for it, anyway. You'll want it to sound its best for the audition. And not one of those stupid little rubber things filled with foam that sucks up a bit of water—those crummy little things people stick in the f-holes thinking they will provide enough moisture through evaporation of about a teaspoon of water. It's so silly, though you have to give the designer top marks for good salesmanship. Get one of those big ones that put a proper amount of moisture in the air of the room where you're keeping it."

"Yes, dear. Tomorrow," Molly replied, used to being nagged to look after her bass by her daughter whose living depended on her instrument being kept in top condition. "I'm already feeling like a quivering bowl of jelly over the audition, so I'll do anything I can to help it go well. Gulp and twitch."

"You'll be just fine, Mother. You were playing very well before you left."

"But three days on the road with no practicing…luckily, my orchestra audition is the same day as the one for the bass teacher. I have three days to work like mad to get back in shape, and then I get it all over with at once," Molly said.

"Call me as soon as you're done to let me know how they went," Shannon said. "And don't forget to take your beta blocker."

"I'm not likely to, with my nerves being in such a state," Molly assured her.

After speaking with Shannon, Molly asked Anthony about a humidifier. He offered to find her one in Tucson when he went in to work the next day. She was relieved and happy Anthony was making life easy for her so she could concentrate on her preparation for the audition. After looking in on Ann and finding her asleep, Molly went to her own room to unpack and make an early night of it.

* * *

Ann slept well and woke refreshed. Remembering the warmth of Anthony's welcome, she felt very much at home and totally relaxed. Anthony's house was large and comfortable, well suited to entertaining long-term guests. Built just outside the boundary of the retirement community at Green Valley, it was all on one level, adobe style, with air conditioning for the summer and a furnace for the winter. The spacious kitchen had a large window overlooking his pool and a good-sized general eating area, making it a natural gathering place. Ann and Molly's bedrooms were in a separate wing of the house where three guest bedrooms were each large enough to accommodate a desk, bed, dresser, and even a television and easy chair. The two bathrooms in this wing were more than sufficient for their needs. This part of the house had been added for the visits of Molly's three children so each could have a bedroom when they came to spend their summer holidays with Anthony and Graham. Decorative security bars covered all the windows and doors. The house was on the path over which many illegal aliens passed from the nearby Mexican border to the city of Tucson.

* * *

Ann was happy to be in Arizona instead of at the seniors' apartment house in Peace River. She enjoyed being spoiled by Anthony, who continued to lavish attention on her, seeing to her every request, making certain she was always comfortable and happy. He cooked special gourmet meals each night, embellished with good California wines Ann had previously refused to drink, claiming they were inferior to her favorite French varieties. He treated her like an honored elder, and she reveled in it.

Anthony's parents had turned their backs on him when he "came out of the closet." They would have no contact with him in spite of his repeated efforts to communicate with them, and died without any reconciliation ever taking place. His disapproving parents had also discouraged his sister from having anything to do with him, and he hadn't seen her since he left home when she was still in primary school. He'd left the country to attend university, taking his first two degrees in Canada at the University of Alberta. A legacy from his grandmother when he reached eighteen supported him until he completed his doctorate. He had finally given up trying to get any response from his family and had no idea where his sister now was, or if he had any living relatives. He was, therefore, delighted to be able to "adopt" Ann and Molly, and the three settled into comfortable domesticity.

Like others of her generation, Ann had preconceived views of gay men, but she was so overwhelmed by Anthony's hospitality, she completely altered her attitudes and opinions and was soon writing letters home to everyone about her delightful new friend. Anthony was not what the straight world thought of as the stereotypical homosexual. He was beginning to lose his hair, and the remaining sparse offering was graying. He sported a relaxed beard and mustache, trimmed but not too carefully shaped. His warm, wide smile and expressive brown eyes convinced most people he found them very special, and in fact, he did. He eschewed the golf most residents of this area played, but swam daily, it being his preferred form of exercise. He was fairly tall and "bearish" in size, as befits a good cook. People of both sexes and orientations were generally drawn to him.

Though Ann had taken to him at once, she was a little concerned about the quantity of alcohol he consumed nightly, which made him poor company as the evening progressed. Still, it hadn't put her off accepting his invitation to return for a visit as soon as she wanted to. She didn't enjoy the Alberta winters, particularly in the years when they were relentlessly cold, and she looked forward to returning to Arizona when its late August heat had abated and the chill of northern Alberta began to set in.

Soon after classes at the university started in September, Molly and Anthony took Ann to the plane. Though they were too busy to see much of her even while she was there, they were sorry to see her go.

Chapter 4

Helene looked at her daughter. She had difficulty believing she was lucky enough to have such a beautiful, bright child. Georgia had always been a happy, carefree kid, easy to bring up.

But something had happened. Georgia had become a stranger. When she looked at Helene at all, it was with hostility and anger. She seemed full of hate. Helene didn't know what she'd done to deserve this kind of treatment. It was devastating.

They used to be able to talk to one another. Now, when Helene tried to find out what was wrong, Georgia only glared at her and walked away. Speech came in monosyllables, the bare minimum response. She wasn't practicing her cello anymore, and when she came home from school, she spent most of the time in her bedroom, with the door locked. Where had her sweet little girl gone? Where was the child who used to come home from school and hold out her arms for a quick hug before rushing off to play with her friends, or read her books, or do her practicing?

Helene wondered if Georgia was missing her friends in Canada. They hadn't had time to say their good-byes when they moved away after her marriage. She'd been overwhelmed when Edwin proposed to her, and married him as soon as school was out in June. She and Georgia had left for Tucson right away.

Because Edwin was a professor at Arizona University, Helene didn't have to pay tuition fees, so as soon as they arrived, she started taking summer school classes. After the struggles she'd gone through to support herself and Georgia for so many years, it seemed miraculous to be able to concentrate on her courses and play in the orchestra without having to work full-time as well.

Maybe that was a mistake. Maybe she wasn't spending enough time with Georgia. Perhaps she should try the direct approach tonight, and just ask Georgia what was wrong, ask her if it would be better if she stayed home instead of spending so much time at classes and orchestra rehearsals. Maybe she'd been too selfish about her own studies.

As Helene thought about the closeness she and Georgia had shared before the move to Arizona, she became more and more homesick for the city they'd left; at least there she had friends to talk to and commiserate with. Why hadn't she kept up her contact with them? Why hadn't she answered Molly's letter? Now she felt so alone. And her husband was no help. Edwin just said Georgia was a typical teenager, it was a stage, she'd get over it. Helene felt tears on her cheeks and wiped them away. She tried to focus her attention on the meal she was making. Maybe Georgia would stay at the dinner table tonight. Helene was making all her favorite foods.

* * *

Georgia felt his hand creeping up the outside of her leg, pushing its way around her thigh…up to her crotch. She pressed her legs more tightly together and moved her chair as far away from him as she could while still being at the table. Her face reflected her revulsion toward this invasion. But nothing she did stopped him. He had arms like an octopus that reached out to grasp at her whenever she was anywhere near him.

Surely Mom knows what he's doing, Georgia thought. Why doesn't she stop it? But if she doesn't know, and I say anything to her, he'll do what he threatened…he'll tell her I'm coming on to him all the time she's away at classes…that I'm asking for it. That I want him.

Georgia practically threw up at the thought. The loathsome man.

When his fingers reached her crotch again, the disgust and hatred she felt for him gave her the strength to jump up from the table and turn to leave the room.

He just smiled that smarmy smile he thought made him look like Mr.-Perfect-Who Never-Does-Anything-Wrong, as her mother returned to the table.

"You should excuse yourself before you leave the table, Georgia." Helene put down the pecan pie as she spoke. "But please come back and finish. I've made your favorite dessert specially."

Georgia turned to her mother, the look she meant for Edwin still on her face, and said angrily, "I'm not hungry." I'd rather starve than sit next to that monster, she wished she could say. Not for ANY dessert will I go back to the table.

Helene thought the look of hatred was directed at her, and tears sprang to her eyes. Her face instantly turned red. Georgia caught the look as she turned to leave the room and felt sorry her mother was hurt, but she couldn't go back. She needed a shower right now, needed to wash away the feeling of filth and shame that overcame her every time her stepfather touched her.

She had to cleanse herself.

It was even worse in the morning. She was leaving the house earlier and earlier, trying to get away before her mom left for classes, so he wouldn't be able to get at her. It was bad enough that every time her mother's back was turned, he reached out and fondled her breasts, and got that knowing look on his face.

Surely Mom's aware of what a slime ball he is, she thought. How much more of this do I have to take before I leave or she stops him?

The shower was hot, and she scrubbed till her skin was nearly raw. Still, she felt dirty.

Georgia went to her room and locked the door. She tried to do her homework but couldn't concentrate. She finally gave up and went to bed, crying herself to sleep.

* * *

Molly marveled at how quickly time had passed. It was the end of September, and she'd already written one set of exams. She looked around the small classroom at the dozen or so other students in this course on twentieth-century composers.

The class had begun with the return of exams. Molly hadn't bothered to open her paper. She was a good student but not a good mark maker, and teachers know there is a big difference. She cherished being totally immersed in the exchange of information that took place, particularly in the seminars. She'd forgotten how much fun it was to be a student, except for those times when you had to take exams and regurgitate whatever you were supposed to have absorbed in your classes. Marks. Mark getting was not going to interfere with her enjoyment of the classes.

"I originally took marks off for non-inclusion of dates of compositions. In the end, since nobody included these dates, as long as you included the date of something directly associated with it, such as its first performance, I realized that at least you had the chronology right, so gave you marks for that," Dr. Hitchmeier explained. He knew most students obsessed over marks. Some would question the professor's judgment of the paper and argue about their marks as if it were a matter of life and death. And in some cases it must seem as if it was. In the present job market, those with the highest marks got the best or only jobs.

The returned paper still in her hand, Molly tuned out. She was lucky her time at the university could be her recreation, her social life, her therapy, so she didn't have to care how Dr. Hitchmeier marked the papers or even if he marked them at all. She'd never been competitive, even as a young student, preferring to let others win the game or get the high marks if it was important to them. She liked to be the one who applauded rather than the one in the limelight. She had no killer instinct.

Being a graduate student was so much better than being an undergraduate. Grads were treated very differently—mainly because they were different, she supposed. Some undergraduates managed to confine their first year at university or college to a survey of the different varieties of beer, how much could be drunk in one evening before they passed out, and how many guys or girls they could go through. Their lab experiments could be said to have consisted of discovering what different kinds of drugs could be ingested safely or otherwise and how little sleep was necessary before it was impossible to make it to classes and exams. The first year away from the relatively controlled atmosphere of home and high school was a total waste for some, and Molly didn't envy them. She thought their activities could be looked upon as an education of sorts—another stage to grow through, to put up with.

A high-school teacher once told Molly, "High school is just a holding tank for kids while they work their way through adolescence." She supposed first-year university was the same for some.

Molly hadn't been involved with the partying groups when she was an undergraduate, nor had she joined the fraternity and sorority crowd. In her opinion, fraternities were for people who needed somebody to choose their friends for them, or didn't have enough to do, or had some prescribed social status to maintain. Though she managed to waste the usual amount of time in her first year, classes, practicing, and rehearsals caused her to confine her social life principally to music students who shared her interests. She, Graham, and Anthony had become close friends during rehearsals and the concert tours their performing groups made to many small communities in Alberta.

Molly was daydreaming when Dr. Hitchmeier's voice invaded her thoughts again. "The mystic chord was used by Scriabin only after 1910. I'm sure I mentioned that several times, so if you didn't mention it, you lost marks." Molly thought the twentieth-century composer Scriabin had done quite a lot with that chord of fourths. Though she wasn't particularly fond of his music, she admired the ingenuity and talent Scriabin exhibited by writing it.

"Missing one or more of the listening examples lost you marks."

Fair. Logical, thought Molly. Anyone with even half a brain could figure that out, but some of the mark grubbers would argue anything if they thought it would get them one extra percent.

"You did well on the Schoenberg."

I guess, thought Molly. Schoenberg is really unmistakable.

"But I wanted you to make a direct connection between the techniques and the piece, not just to list the techniques, so you lost marks if you didn't make the connection."

Grad school classes. Where professors actually expected you to think. Molly's thoughts drifted to Anthony. He was still grieving for Graham, who had died of complications related to AIDS. When Graham Winslow joined Anthony in Arizona and never returned to his family, she had not seen him again, though she heard news of him through the children and exchanged phone calls with him about the children's travels back and forth for holidays.

Long ago, Molly had forgiven both Graham and Anthony for the breakup of her marriage and the heartbreak of having her husband, the father of her children, leave her for a man, and their mutual friend at that. It had seemed to her, after the initial shock, just too preposterous, so she directed her energy into making sure the family survived—Graham's parents as well as his children. Through sheer determination, she helped everyone accept their changed circumstances and learned to live with the new order.

Now Molly and Anthony both needed help to carry on after the loss of their partners. At least she would always have her children and extended family, while poor Anthony had no one.

She sighed, and tried to focus on the class.

"Any comments on the Hindemith biography by the guest lecturer?"

Dr. Hitchmeier was already embarking upon a new topic, the exam having been fully dealt with.

Hands went up.

"I found it fascinating, the way the hermit just wanted to meditate, the artist just wanted to paint, and the composer just wanted to write music...how they all, in their own very different times, were being pressured to be socially conscious. The way it was all tied together in Hindemith's opera *Mathis der Maler*." The young man who responded first was always excited about twentieth-century composers, no matter how difficult they were to listen to. Molly suspected he was a closet composer himself.

"I still don't quite understand 'musical hermeneutics,' but I really enjoyed seeing the paintings and hearing all about her research," another student carefully offered.

"We didn't get much of musical hermeneutics in her lecture," Dr. Hitchmeier responded. "She had to set up every step of the presentation, bring the information together, and summarize it for us, and there wasn't time to get to the hermeneutics."

Molly tuned out again. She had enjoyed the lecture by the visiting expert, but thought Hindemith's music was nasty. She could appreciate the mind of the person who created it, but she didn't like it. She'd decided to register for this class to enlarge her knowledge and experience, and hoped the outcome for her would be a greater appreciation and enjoyment of modern music. So far it had increased her appreciation intellectually, but hadn't done much for her aesthetic enjoyment. She felt at least she was giving it a chance, so she could heartily dislike whatever she wanted to, without guilt. Many of the Romantic composers wrote sentimental trash that also left her cold, so she didn't really expect to learn to like all twentieth-century music either.

Dr. Hitchmeier was explaining to the class why another speaker they'd had the previous week had been a poor choice.

"I won't say I was told Mr. Hegsky must be given a forum in this class, but...." He opened his hands and held them out as he hunched and shrugged his shoulders. The class got the point.

Regula, one of Molly's classmates, leaned over to whisper to her. "That weasel, Dean Kaiser, pushing Dr. Hitchmeier around again, using his position to get rid of unwanted guests, shoving them off to nice, gentle Hitchmeier because he wouldn't make waves. The dean has no backbone—he should have refused this man altogether."

The guest was touted as an authority in the Russian musical world. He'd exhibited this authority by writing a string of Russian composers' names on the board and, while the resident Russian professor translated, spent the rest of the class time being political, occasionally referring to composers in order to make it seem legitimate for him to take their class time to expound his political views.

"Just as he shouldn't have shoved the orchestra conductor on us...we'll probably never get rid of the guy," Helene, on the other side of Molly, snorted. Molly looked at her fondly. Making contact with Helene, finding they were both taking this course and playing in the same orchestra together, had been the high point of Molly's fall term. So far they'd only been able to see one another at these times, Helene's schedule being too full to allow for any visits apart from those snatched before and after their classes and rehearsals.

Molly allowed herself to tune out again. She remembered how surprised some people had been when she "allowed" the children to visit their father in Arizona for holidays. They were sure the children would be tainted by his influence, which amused Molly greatly. As if being gay were an infectious disease, an attitude Molly considered a holdover from the Middle Ages. Even some of her supposedly liberal-thinking friends had been aghast at her acceptance of her first husband's orientation and his defection to his lover.

She couldn't pretend she hadn't sometimes been very resentful, as if Graham could help being what he was. Molly remembered frantically filling her life with activity to try to overcome her shock. She certainly spent many sleepless nights hating the two of them, nights filled with tears, feeling sorry for herself, mourning the loss of the comfortable life they had shared as a family. Healing was possible only after she accepted the fact that she was wasting her emotions on something she couldn't change.

And now Graham was gone...Anthony was left. Paul was gone...Molly was left. She almost smiled as she thought of them as the two leftovers, together in Arizona. Despite the oddness of the triangle in which they'd been involved, it had been amazingly easy to resume their old undergraduate friendship.

Many of Molly's acquaintances had questioned her decision to spend the year at Anthony's so soon after her husband's death. As if it were shocking, with inexplicable sexual implications. She had often found herself incapable of controlling her laughter at their awkwardly expressed concerns.

She'd been relieved Graham's family understood her need to go away. They'd managed to forgive Graham and Anthony many years ago, though it had been difficult and painful for them. Now that Patrick Jr. was being primed to run the eminently successful Winslow family business they'd hoped Graham would eventually take over, they were appeased. Patrick and his grandfather were so inseparable it had been difficult to pry him loose to go to visit his father during the school breaks. He grudgingly accepted the compromise of half-and-half holidays, and Graham had been satisfied. He'd had his daughters' friendship. They had adored their father, and Molly was glad she had not prevented their regular visits.

The next time she tuned in to the class, one of the students was doing a presentation about Berg. Molly was still holding her test paper and had not yet even looked at it.

"Berg's Lyric Suite is a work for string quartet."

"If we didn't already know that, we shouldn't be in the class," Helene complained to Molly.

"Berg annotated a copy of the work. The notes showed it clearly had a programmatic component. It was about a lady with whom he was having a love affair, a lady who was not his wife." The presenter looked coy. "Both the lover and his wife had names starting with H. Of course, you all know the letter 'H' is B-natural in music."

Molly was becoming irritated. She wished he would get on with it.

"The bottom line is this. You can come up with…." Molly's ears went into deaf mode yet again. She'd been "bottom-lined" to death in previous student presentations and wished she hadn't come to today's class. She had a suspicion it was going to be a washout, judging from the fellow's previous classroom presentation, and wished the professor would do all the "presenting" himself. From his wide experience, he knew many good stories about the composers and performers, and his lectures were very interesting as well as informative.

Helene turned to Molly and whispered, "Earth to Molly. Earth to Molly. Aren't you going to look at your exam? We finished dealing with it fifteen minutes ago."

Molly glanced down at the paper in her hand—96%. She was surprised, although she had known all the answers. As an undergrad, she had often been marked down for not padding her answers with details not asked for, a practice she strenuously objected to, instead of concisely answering the question. It seemed to be a lot easier to make marks in graduate school. Maybe these professors didn't have time to read fillers. She certainly hadn't added any.

Or maybe, in all her years of living since undergraduate days, she'd changed, become more focused—unlike today, when she was in another world during most of the class.

"Professor Hitchmeier should tell them he's taking marks off if the presentation exceeds the fifteen-minute limit," Helene whispered indignantly. "Then they'd be darn sure not to take so long."

Molly agreed, and then let her thoughts drift away again, this time to her bass audition. She had played well enough that Dr. Gerhardt agreed to take her on as a student, and Dr. Sneazewell let her into the orchestra, his only comment at the conclusion of her audition being a grunt. She was sure her success was thanks to the beta blocker she'd used. The lessons were great, but she was ambivalent about the orchestra. She enjoyed playing the music, but was constantly irritated by the conductor. She considered him a boor—though a brilliant boor. Luckily, liking the conductor wasn't a prerequisite for playing in an orchestra.

Molly shook herself to bring her attention back to the twentieth-century music class. The next student was making a presentation on Stravinsky.

"'L'Histoire du soldat' is not the correct way to say the title. The piece was originally just 'Soldier's Story.' Stravinsky never used the L' at the beginning of the title. During the political upheavals in Russia, Stravinsky was forced to find a new publisher and the British one he chose decided he knew French better than Stravinsky, so he added the article. But Stravinsky never did. However, it has stuck. But I just say, 'Histoire soldat,' and that is why, in case you were wondering."

We weren't, thought Molly uncharitably.

He went on. "Stravinsky went to law school. He never did study music formally. Rimsky-Korsakov advised him not to go to the conservatory, as it would confine him too much. Instead, he suggested Stravinsky study with one of Rimsky-Korsakov's students, and then later himself, so as not to be limited.

"The war cut him off from Russia and the financial support of his family, and he eventually went to live in Switzerland. Due to the ravages of war, they came upon a period of necessity for musical economy. The large orchestras were too expensive. People couldn't afford them. He decided he needed to write pieces that could easily travel, with only a few musicians and performers being required.

"Stravinsky wanted to write music that would appeal to every man in every country. He didn't like attending a concert where everyone behaved as if it was a holy ritual, a religious experience, where you had to bow down to the 'Almighty Composer'—like Wagner. He didn't like the musicians being stuck in the pit. Stravinsky wanted his pieces to be read, danced and played on stage, the arts all interrelated, even the movements of the musicians becoming part of the story."

Molly tried to look attentive while her mind wandered in and out of her classmate's narrative. At least some of this was interesting stuff, but off the fifteen-minute presentation topic they had been assigned. She noticed the other students were becoming restless, too.

"This guy is a dweeb. He's wasting our time rambling on about the plot of 'Histoire soldat.' We all know the plot," Helene complained.

"Oh, well, we must be kind to our fellow students," Molly whispered back, although she'd missed the entire plot review while she daydreamed. "We can always meditate on something else while he drones on...which," she admitted, "was precisely what I was doing."

"I don't feel kind, and I'm getting angry," Helene whispered back. "I wish he'd get on with it."

Molly tuned back to the presentation to hear, "Stravinsky thought of the instruments as being in four families—winds, strings, brass, and multiple percussion, which he regarded as another unique family, rather than just a color instrument group—each instrumentalist a soloist all the time."

Returning to her private thoughts, Molly composed her face to look interested. Today she just didn't care about Stravinsky, or the class, but she didn't want to hurt the poor child's feelings.

Chapter 5

As the class hour neared its end, Molly's thoughts turned to the reactions of people she, as an older student, had met at the university. She found them fascinating, and thought they would be a good thesis subject if she were in psychology. Because she was in the "old lady" classification as far as most students were concerned, they thought she was on the faculty. When they found out she was a student, some became quite uncomfortable. They didn't know what to make of her, whether to treat her the same way they treated their mothers' friends, dancing around the edge and escaping as soon as possible, or as a bona fide student. Others managed very well, and she discovered, as she got to know them, that they came from families where conversation across the generations was a common occurrence.

Most of the students in her classes and the orchestra had become used to her and seemed to enjoy her company. Their enthusiasm and animated conversation helped her when she was missing her own children.

Molly took advantage of the students who regard older people as deaf or just not there by quite unrepentantly listening in to their conversations. She often overheard things they would never have said if they hadn't forgotten she was there, including some references to Anthony she would rather not have heard. One bitter young man, who had not received the scholarship he was sure he deserved, referred to him as the "gay drunk," and Molly had been shocked and hurt for Anthony. She resolved to find a time to confront him about his drinking.

The responses of some of the faculty to her advanced age presented her with more opportunities to reflect on their personalities. Her orchestra conductor, Dr. Sneazewell, whom she considered a tiresome little man, ignored her as she sat where he'd placed her at the end of her section. She was no match for most of these young superstar students and was happy where she was. She was also thankful he did not consider her important enough to include in the roster of regulars to whom he directed his continuous line of offensive insults. She heard he could be very charming, but she hadn't seen that side of him yet.

Apart from his obnoxious personality, Dr. Sneazewell was a brilliant musician and could not be faulted on his knowledge of the scores and his interpretive skills. She wondered why he hadn't made it in the bigger world. Many conductors routinely got away with insulting professional musicians, but maybe it didn't work on the guest conductor circuit. She suspected many musicians refused to play under his baton, and she knew whole orchestras had ways they could foil a conductor if they hated him enough.

Molly greatly enjoyed her bass teacher, Dr. Gerhardt, a sweet and kind-hearted man. Very little of her lesson was spent playing for him. Most of the time they discussed pedagogy. He talked about what he felt should be included in students' technique and development from the very beginning. Since he'd never taught students as young as those with whom Molly worked, he asked many questions about her teaching. As a result, they both looked forward to the weekly lesson, trading advice and information on repertoire, technique, and order of presentation. They looked on each other as colleagues rather than as teacher and student.

Molly was forced to tune back into the present as Helene poked her and said, "It's over. You can leave now. And for heaven's sake, take that indulgent smile off your face. You look as though you were watching one of your children perform. And don't try to tell me this class wasn't a waste of your time today. You were really out of it. I'm ashamed of you."

"I'm sorry, Helene." Molly was duly chastised. "Did I embarrass you with my slide off into la-la land? Usually I love my time here, and listen avidly."

"And so you should. It upsets me to see anyone waste these classes." Helene was becoming unusually emotional, and it startled Molly.

"Yes, yes,...I know I've let the geriatric set down by being inattentive. But today I couldn't get myself focused. I hope I can get my brain functioning for the orchestra rehearsal, or I'll be getting creative in my bowing. It's tough enough as it is trying to follow the principal bass's markings," she said as she gathered up her things. "Wouldn't Sneazy like that! He'd probably make a nasty comment about the old musician who needs a vitamin fix to keep up with her section."

"Well, I always feel we're so lucky to be here," Helene continued berating Molly as if she hadn't heard the reply. "And there's something to be learned from everything. When tests are returned and the professor discusses them, I find out new things, angles I missed. And even the kids' presentations give me a new slant on the person they're talking about. These young people are like a breath of fresh air, even though I do sometimes get annoyed when they go on too long."

"Yes, yes, Helene. I get it. Don't nag. You're forgetting I'm an old school teacher, too," Molly replied. Beginning to feel a bit miffed at her friend's outburst, she snapped back, "And why do you care whether or not I pay attention, anyway?"

"Because you're my friend, and I hate to see you wasting your time." Helene's eyes were blazing. She turned her back on Molly, picked up her books, and rushed out the door. Molly stood looking after her for a minute, wondering what had set her off, why she was so touchy. Usually Helene was a such a good-natured, easy-going person. She gathered up her own books and followed her out the door slowly.

Molly and Helen had only one brief contact by phone before the first class. Now they snatched visits walking from class to the orchestra rehearsal that followed. They hadn't yet found time to have a proper visit. Maybe she should make time.

A contrite Helene was waiting down the hall for Molly. "I guess I have no right to nag you. I'm sorry. Things aren't so great for me at home these days, so I'm more irritable than usual. I'm not sure how long I'll be able to enjoy my university life, and I find myself being overly protective of it while I'm here."

"What's wrong? I thought you were happy here. Is it the usual second marriage adjustment?" Molly asked. Their short conversations so far had been devoted to their courses, so they hadn't discussed what was going on in their private lives.

"No. I'll talk to you about it another day. Right now we've got to get moving. If we don't get to orchestra on time, that egotistical little snot will have something more to get into a rage over," Helene said, and they hastened down the hallway to the instrument storage lockers located near the rehearsal room. "I love the music, but Sneazewell gives me the creeps."

Molly didn't allow herself to daydream in the orchestra. She loved playing, and really had to keep her wits about her as she tackled the repertoire. One of the pieces on which they were working, Beethoven's Fifth Symphony, with its marvelous rhythmic opening, was so well known by even the most casual concert-goer that rehearsals were tense. Dr. Sneazewell seemed determined to make the eventual performance an outstanding aesthetic experience for the audience, even though he was working with a student orchestra. Molly hoped her practice sessions would help her to achieve the lightness and speed necessary for the scherzo. The whole symphony was a love-in for bass players, whose part was elegant, though difficult, all the way through.

In spite of Dr. Sneazewell's personality defects, orchestra was Molly's favorite class, and she looked forward to the two-hour rehearsals three days a week. The only part she didn't like was hauling the bass about. It was the only time she ever wished she played a different instrument, such as a flute or, she shuddered, a violin. The rehearsals were generally excellent, except for the conductor's insults.

And this rehearsal was no exception.

"Shall we give you a tuning fork for each pitch so you can get your notes in tune?" Dr. Sneazewell asked one poor string player near the beginning. "Or are you so deaf you don't know you're out of tune?" Then he licked his finger and flipped over a page of his score, as if he were flinging the offending musician off the stage.

"That had the sensitivity of a smelly sport sock." He directed this comment at the woodwind section, completely ignoring the dark looks shot his way in response. Sneazewell, as usual, then licked his finger, grasped the page of music, and flung it over to register his disgust at the musicians' inadequacies.

"Your fortes are so anemic they sound as if you need a blood transfusion," he growled at the whole orchestra. Lick. Fling.

"You're walking through this piece as if you had a stick up your bum," was his next insult, one of the milder of his often crude comments.

"And you, Laskin, shouldn't even pretend to be playing any instrument," he said to the assistant principal cellist. "Rhythmically, you'd give even the worst percussion student heartburn."

"Cranbrook, such an ugly sound should be outlawed. Whoever gave you the idea you should play an instrument?" he said scornfully. "Maybe you should try mud wrestling, or football. Perhaps your sensitivity could aspire to that level." Sneazewell paused and glared contemptuously at his victim. "No, not even that sensitive." Lick. Fling.

"Miss Holburn, your advanced years do not give you the right to daydream in my rehearsal. Your playing is barely good enough to grant you a chair in this orchestra," he said as he looked down the section to the second violinist. "And don't think I haven't seen you batting your eyes at the brasses. They'll never fall for it, dear. I suggest you put blinkers on, and save your energy for your music and your stand partner." Agatha Holburn was also the librarian for the orchestra. She looked back at him with disgust and loathing. Had he not already returned his attention to the score, he might have seen a warning in those piercing eyes. He missed altogether the sympathetic look her stand partner, his wife, gave her, and the look Jolene directed his way after she had commiserated with Agatha.

"You sound like an overage contralto. I've tried, but I really can't figure out what pitch you are actually trying to find. For heaven's sake, tighten up your vibrato, you miserable musical misfit." His next thrust was directed at Trent Quillium in the cello section.

"He wouldn't try that on any of the professionals," Helene said to Molly as she wrapped her viola in its case at the end of the rehearsal. "I'm surprised he hasn't been bumped off. He's been picking on Trent Quillium and Agatha Holburn since the first rehearsal, almost as if he had a personal vendetta. Probably they're both struggling financially to afford to stay in university and depend on his evaluation for their loans and work scholarships. He's the kind who would make it his business to know who's vulnerable and can't answer back." She closed her viola case carefully, settled the carrying strap over her shoulder, and continued chatting while she waited for Molly to finish the more labor-intensive job of packing up her bass.

"I'm sure the thought of murder has occurred to them many times," Molly replied as she slid the heavy canvas case over the scroll at the top of the bass and pulled it down over the side. "I'd hate to be trapped into having to take the crap old Sleazy dishes out. He's just an ego surrounded by flesh. His little ritual of licking his finger and turning a page, then doing the same thing several times just after he attacks someone is so revolting. Maybe he takes nasty pills just before the rehearsal. He seems to get more virulent as it goes on." Molly pulled savagely on the zipper until it was far enough down that she could lay the bass on its side to zip around the bottom of the instrument.

Helene giggled. "Nasty pills? That's the best excuse I've heard yet. Have you noticed, though, he doesn't try his nasties on the principals of the sections. He knows he has the wannabes under his thumbs, but he also knows he'd better not rile the best ones or they might transfer to another university and then he'd be in hot water. I also notice he leaves the bass section alone completely," Helene concluded.

"It's because they're short of basses this year and, anyway, to most conductors, bass players aren't musicians. They're only noticed if they make really appalling mistakes or play too loudly. In conductors' minds, we're just there to do the drone work," Molly replied resentfully as she continued packing, stowing away her music, bow, and rosin in the little pockets strategically positioned on the case.

"I'm surprised someone hasn't throttled Sneazy with that silly towel he wears around his neck. He's so theatrical, the way he uses it to wipe the sweat from his brow as he conducts. Or maybe somebody will get mad enough to spear him with his own baton someday. We'll all cheer," Helene added as they left the rehearsal room.

Molly returned her bass to the oversized locker.

"I'm tempted to try to rent a bass to leave here for orchestra and lessons so I can keep this one at home to practice, instead of hauling it back and forth on weekends," she said as she struggled to settle the giant into her locker.

"What are you whining about? You have a wheel for your bass. It's not as if you had to carry it everywhere," Helene reminded her. "And don't try to kid me. There's no way you'd use a lesser quality instrument."

"It's still such a pain having to remove the end pin to replace it with the wheel and make sure it's tightly screwed on so it doesn't wobble. You almost need a driving course to steer the wheel, once you get it on." Molly sighed. "I guess I'm just getting lazier as I get older. But you're right. This instrument is precious to me, even though it's a no-name old bass. I love its beautiful, dark sound. And it's smaller than most three-quarter-size basses, so even my pudgy fingers can articulate the notes."

The string length on basses and violas determines what size they're designated. It's crucial, if the musician has two instruments, to make sure the string length is the same so the distances between pitches are the same. The shorter the string length, the closer the notes are to each other, and short-fingered Molly was lucky to have one that not only had a beautiful tone, but also was the right size for the span of her hand. The distance between her first and fourth fingers was perfect for this bass, and she was comfortable playing it.

"You have such a wonderfully large hand, Helene. I envy you being able to play your big viola. It has such a rich sound."

Helene hugged her instrument and agreed she was lucky. Molly gathered up her books from the locker, and the two friends made their way down the hall to smaller lockers where Helene picked up her books, keeping her viola with her.

"Back to Sneazewell, and Agatha Holburn," Helene said as they started for the car park. "I found out she gets back at him by saying they can't get music he wants. I think he suspects that's what she's doing, but he's too lazy to check it out. His wife is a great friend of Agatha's, which must really gall him."

"He sure has mood swings," Molly said. "He's either high as a kite or in the depths of despair and taking it out on people in the orchestra. I wonder if he has a serious psychological problem."

"You haven't been cured yet of trying to psychoanalyze or make excuses for people, have you?" Helene laughed at her friend. "You're always trying to find reasons why some people are disasters. You're a walking psychology book."

"Well, I can't really believe people are happy when they're being deliberately mean and vicious to others. Frankly, he sounds manic depressive to me."

"Don't even try to explain the man. I just wish they'd replace him. I'm glad we're older students and not vulnerable enough for him to pick on—at least I suspect that's why he leaves us alone."

"It's nice to be ignored, I agree. But I still have difficulty listening to him annihilate these kids and humiliate them in front of everyone. And poor Agatha Holburn just doesn't deserve the treatment he metes out to her," Molly continued as they entered the parking lot. "But, changing the subject to you, Helene, what's up? What's happening with your new family? Why might you not be here much longer?"

"I don't think you even want to know what I suspect is going wrong in my family," Helene said, "and I don't want to hear any psychological claptrap and excuses for the behavior of my not-so-new husband, the former big love-of-my-life."

"If someone is treating you badly, I will find no excuse for him. I will kill him with my own bare hands," Molly said firmly.

"If what I have begun to think is true, I may do that myself."

By this time they were at Molly's car.

"So, what DO you suspect?" Molly insisted.

"I can't talk now. I've got to rush." Helene began hurrying away to her car.

"Wait, Helene. You can't leave without telling me more," Molly said, trying to detain her.

"No time. Gotta go," and Helene was out of sight around the next row of cars.

Molly looked after her, frustrated, wondering if Helene thought she was doing Molly a favor by not confiding in her. Didn't she realize Molly would worry until they met again, and not even know what she was worrying about?

* * *

Molly drove out of the car park thinking how odd it was Helene hadn't ever talked to her about her husband or her daughter since she'd arrived. Being too wrapped up in her own life to notice Helene's silence, Molly realised she hadn't even asking any questions about them, and that was unlike her. She still hadn't met Edwin, though he worked at the university. It was such a huge place, it was easy to miss people even in the same faculty, and Edwin never seemed to be around the university when Helene was.

As she gained the freeway and left the city, the beauty of the desert drive distracted Molly from her concern for Helene. She wondered how she could ever have thought it would be a boring place to live. The mountains surrounding the area appeared to enclose it like a huge fort. The regal saguaro cacti stood like beacons, and the prickly pear reminded her of a bunch of avocado pancakes. The big treelike mesquite had a very dark bark, and the cholla looked like teddy bears, so soft and cuddly you think you would like to hug them. Never a good idea.

The cacti were not sprouting their magical flowers, but she was satisfied with their present beauty. For her, they didn't need flowers. No matter how negative and nasty Dr. Sneazewell had been in rehearsal, her spirits lifted each night during the thirty-minute drive to Green Valley from the university in Tucson. Clouds in the darkening skies burst into many colors and patterns, as the sun disappeared behind the mountains. She was treated to a different performance every night.

Sometimes the euphoria she felt suddenly evaporated, and feelings of guilt, fear, and sadness overtook her. Guilt because she was alive, enjoying herself, being happy...and Paul was dead. It should not have been Paul lying there in that pool of blood. He should be the one driving along enjoying the sunset. She tried to tell herself feeling guilty wasn't going to bring him back to life. Maybe there was a reason she was still alive. Maybe there was something she still had to do in this world.

The sunset disappeared quickly, reminding Molly life's joys were fleeting and not to be passed by without notice or clouded by guilt. She hoped wherever Paul's spirit was now, it was at peace...if that's what spirits experienced after death. Since she couldn't know for sure until she had, as her family said, "dropped off" herself, she decided there wasn't much point in speculating about it. She turned her thoughts to the job of negotiating the traffic, as yet another enormous truck passed her even though she was driving at a little over the speed limit herself.

* * *

He's done it again, Trent thought. The bastard manages to make me look like a silly incompetent every rehearsal. I know I'm a good cellist, but he reduces me to rubble with one well chosen insult. Sure, he told himself, I'm not the only one he picks on, but his remarks to me are the most demeaning. He knows how they hurt. Why does he do it? Why doesn't somebody do something about him? Why don't I do something about him?

Because I'm a weak-willed, lily-livered coward, that's why.

Trent found he was having many conversations with himself as he became more and more alienated from the rest of the students in the orchestra. He was so demoralized after each rehearsal he would slink off to his cello case, wrap the instrument up carelessly, and sidle out of the rehearsal hall with his head down, neither seeing nor hearing attempts made by some of the more kind members of orchestra to commiserate with him. He returned each day to his dreary room and lay on his bed, neither practicing nor composing, drained of any desire to do something productive. He stared at the ceiling, thinking up ways to get rid of his enemies. Dr. Sneazewell, the conductor, was at the top of the list. He replayed every insult in his mind, thinking of all the retorts he should have made, wishing he could have thought of them at the time, and knowing that, even if he had, he didn't have the courage to voice them. Sneazewell had too much power and could fail him in that class. He couldn't afford failure. Unless he gave up altogether...and he wasn't quite there yet.

* * *

As she lay in bed, Ruby thought about her most recent encounter with Anthony Clint. Dr. Clint. Big deal chair of the department. She'd get him. She thought she'd probably made a little more headway this time—after a few more well directed attacks, he'd be forced to give her some scholarship money. And once she had the money in her hands, she'd deal with Sneazewell, who was getting just a little tiresome. He wasn't nearly as good as he thought he was. At anything. Except, maybe, making love.

Love. She snorted. Sneazewell didn't know the meaning of the word. Let's just call it what it really is. Sex. Copulation. Fornication. Whatever.

Ruby turned over in bed to look at her current husband, Dick Jensen. He was sleeping like a baby, and in many ways that's just what he was. She lightly stroked the long, luxuriant hair he usually wore in a ponytail.

The opposite of Sneazewell, Dick was useful. He would do anything she asked of him. Not enormously bright, but convenient and easily manipulated most of the time. She'd learned her lesson. Use or be used.

Too bad his work was centered in this area. She would have preferred going to a different university and missing the Sneazewell connection.

Ruby suddenly felt the need for a drink. Would it never leave her? She got up and took a sleeping pill. By the time she fell asleep, she'd figured out five more ways to scare Anthony into giving her money.

* * *

"I notice you're getting a little too friendly with your stand partner in the orchestra," Lance Sneazewell said imperiously as he cut into the steak—filet mignon, rare—he insisted upon every night. He claimed it was because Jolene didn't know how to cook anything else, but she knew it was really because he'd grown up with nothing, certainly not steak, and especially not the beef tenderloin she bought all the time.

"Really, Lance," Jolene replied, summoning up an indignant voice. "What could possibly upset you about my friendship with that mouse Agatha?"

"You look like a couple of lesbians, that's what," he roared. "Chatting and giggling in the back row. I won't have my wife treating rehearsals without the proper respect and decorum. Don't think I don't notice what you're up to…."

So what's wrong with lesbians? Jolene thought. The more of you I see, the more attractive the idea becomes. You look disgusting, chewing with your big mouth open like that. She couldn't imagine why she used to think it was a sensuous mouth, or why the thought of it touching her had made her quiver with delight. She remembered how impressed she had been when he first noticed her and made her feel so special. Maybe it was because she was so far away from home. At the time, he had made her feel cherished and protected.

"You can't have it both ways, Lance," Jolene ventured to cut into his tirade to say. "Agatha and I are either lesbians or, as you said at the rehearsal, she's batting her eyes at the brass section."

Lance, as usual, did not bother to answer his wife, but continued as if she hadn't spoken at all.

"...in the rear of the section, which is where you've shown you belong more and more."

Jolene tuned out the old windbag. If his colleagues and admirers could see the way he behaved at home, they wouldn't be nearly so impressed. She should have wondered about his previous marriages before she married him. But that's like thinking, when one of the strings on your violin breaks in the middle of your recital, you should have worked in a new set long before. Too late to fix.

But it wasn't too late. She was biding her time.

Jolene heard nothing of the rest of Lance Sneazewell's continuing tirade as she watched him finish his meal. Retreating to her own thoughts was the way she survived. He never minded her silence. He was used to being in charge, holding forth, and insulting everyone and everything.

"You overdid my steak," he said, as he pushed his chair away from the table.

Jolene was not surprised this was his only acknowledgment of her preparation of the food. He managed to find fault with everything she did. He considered his complaint a fitting end to each meal.

Chapter 6

When Molly saw Helene at her locker the next day, she suggested they have lunch at the cafeteria before the next twentieth-century music class. Molly had been worried about Helene since the previous orchestra rehearsal, but didn't feel she should phone and intrude. Helene had always been a private person who didn't like to be pushed into divulging her personal problems. Maybe if she shared her own, Helene might loosen up.

"Anthony has really been worrisome." Molly slumped down next to Helene in a secluded corner of the cafeteria with her sandwich and cup of tea. "If AIDS doesn't get him, the liquor will." She sighed.

"My father was an alcoholic," Helene confided, unwrapping her own sandwich. "My mom and I started going to Al-Anon. It's a support group for friends and families of alcoholics. They helped us try to understand and accept my dad as an alcoholic. Mom managed to quit feeling responsible for his drinking. They're both dead now, but I still go to meetings occasionally. Do you want me to take you to one?"

"Thanks, Helene, I would," Molly replied.

The two ate hungrily. When they'd finished, Molly said, "Now we have some time, please tell me what's happening. I've worried about you all weekend."

"I don't know if I have a real problem or if I'm imagining things."

"It might help to talk about it."

"I don't know, Molly. Sometimes you're such a babe in the woods, I'm not sure you'd understand." Helene's misery was palpable.

"I can learn, Helene." Molly leaned over and took one of Helene's hands. "Please give me a chance."

Helene shrugged and took a deep breath. "I suppose it's worth a try, and at least you're discreet. I suspect my supposedly wonderful husband is either working up to, or may already be, sexually abusing my thirteen-year-old daughter." Tears filled Helene's eyes.

Molly's face betrayed her shock. She drew in her breath sharply. It was a moment before she could reply.

"The last time I saw Georgia was in Edmonton, just before you left. At twelve years old, she was already a beautiful girl. I'm sure most men would admire her."

"She is gorgeous, and a wonderful daughter, too," Helene assured her. "Up until this year we've always been very close."

"I've not met your husband, so I don't know what kind of person he is, or what to suggest," Molly responded. "I'm sorry we didn't get a chance to meet him before you married."

"I was so busy arranging to leave, I didn't have time to talk to anyone. And I thought you'd all disapprove, since I hadn't known Edwin that long. He wanted me to marry him right away. I was really flattered. He's such a handsome man, and I'm a big woman. Men are usually put off by fat. It was all terribly romantic." Helene took a sip of her coffee and groaned. "Now, as I think back on it, I wonder if he started being very attentive when he met me with my daughter. I had her over at the university one day soon after my classes began. I'm beginning to wonder if it was really Georgia he was after, not me. That's an awful thing to think about your husband."

"Not awful, Helene. It's a realistic mother protecting her baby chick," Molly replied. "What is he doing that makes you suspect this?"

"I haven't seen him doing anything, so it's not so much what he's doing, as what's happening to Georgia. We used to be good friends. She used to be a happy girl who really enjoyed school. We used to do things together, to talk to one another a lot. Now she's become morose. She hardly ever talks to me or to Edwin, just eyes us both with hostility. And lately, when I have orchestra rehearsals, she's taken to staying over at her friend's house. I've phoned to check on her, and she's always there, and the friend's mother says she loves having her there, but she won't talk to me about anything."

"Those symptoms could be that old jerk, Mother Nature, making adolescence a painful time for kids and their parents. But they could also be what you suspect. Have you talked to Edwin?"

"He just says she's being a typical teenager and she'll grow out of it. But he's divorced, and his first wife has full custody of their daughters somewhere in the East. He never sees them. I doubt he knows anything about teenagers."

"Why were they divorced?"

"We haven't talked about his first marriage. He doesn't seem to want to, and I don't push it. I don't particularly care to talk about mine, either," she added, and took another sip of her coffee. "There are other disturbing things, though. She went out and bought a lock for her bedroom door and keeps it locked. I've never gone through her stuff and she's never accused me of it, so why does she feel the need to lock her door? I don't know what brought that on. And she's been 'forgetting' things, like leaving used pads in the bathroom. It's kind of creepy." The tears were now spilling out of Helene's eyes and rolling unnoticed down her cheeks. "And I never seem to have time alone with her, long enough to have a good talk. Either she has to leave for school right away in the mornings, or Edwin's already home when I get there after classes. He has a lighter teaching load this semester and short hours."

"It doesn't sound too good, Helene. What about taking Georgia away from the house, just the two of you? How about a shopping trip to a place where Edwin wouldn't want to go, or at a time when he's busy at the university? Even if it means you have to miss one of your classes and take Georgia out of school for a day. Or just bring her over to Anthony's place, or anywhere you can talk alone without being interrupted."

"Maybe I'll try that. Edwin does all the shopping. I have no income down here. He pays all the bills, and we're both dependent on him. My university tuition and benefits are looked after because he's on faculty, everything here is his. I can't use shopping as an excuse unless I ask him for money, so that won't do. I will take you up on your offer if I don't think of something else." Molly found a tissue and wiped the tears from Helene's cheeks. Helene continued to speak as if she hadn't noticed her friend's ministrations. "I don't know what I'm going to do if marrying Edwin turns out to be a mistake. I don't know why I've allowed myself to become so dependent. I have no other resources. It puts me at his mercy, so I feel guilty about being suspicious of him when he's been so good to us, materially."

"Listen, Helene, don't let money matters keep you with Edwin if things aren't good. You know you can depend on me for any help you need, financial or otherwise. If you really think these things are happening, get away from it now, before it's too late, and damn the rest. Nothing is as important as your daughter's welfare. If you even suspect something is wrong, you have to protect her." Molly had become increasingly tense and suspicious as Helene continued to talk, and now was beginning to feel almost frantic.

Helene caught the urgency in Molly's voice. "Look, Molly, you have your own worries. I don't want you to have to load this on your pile, too. I'll go home and watch carefully. If I still think something's going on, and I need help, I'll call you."

"Don't leave it too long, Helene. Your daughter's too important. Promise you'll call me, for sure," Molly insisted. Helene assured her she would.

* * *

In the days following, Helene wouldn't talk about her problem again. It was as if she was embarrassed she had mentioned it to Molly at all. Then major upheavals in Molly's life with Anthony consumed all her attention.

Since arriving in Arizona, Molly had watched Anthony getting drunk before bedtime most nights. It didn't make sense to her. He was bright, successful in his career, full of energy, and had always been pretty active. The loss of Graham and the continuous fear of AIDS probably contributed to his depression. Still, she hadn't had much to do with him since their university days, when so many of them seemed to her to drink too much, so she really didn't know his drinking habits. The kids had never mentioned anything when they returned from spending their holidays with Graham and Anthony.

"When did you start drinking so much, Anthony?" she asked, the evening after her lunch with Helene.

"Don't bug me, Molly. I've had a hard year." He looked at his glass, now empty yet again.

"Tell me about it," Molly replied, hoping he would open up to her.

"I don't want to trouble you with my problems," Anthony said, getting up to refill his empty glass.

"And anyway, there's nothing you can do. Graham's gone and I've had it. You must have realized that if Graham had AIDS, I'd be next."

"Do you have AIDS yet? Or are you just HIV-positive?"

"JUST positive? You must be kidding. JUST." He laughed in a haunted way. "Yes, I'm JUST positive."

"But doesn't that mean your immune system is still working? That you may have many years left?"

"Many years. And all of them without Graham." He was seriously depressed, and Molly could see the drink was not helping. It was just feeding the depression. "You know what I'm talking about," he continued. "How are you dealing with the fact that you must face life without Paul?"

Molly thought for a moment before replying. She didn't want to hurt Anthony, but she might as well tell him.

"When Graham left me for you so many years ago, I did what seemed a lifetime of crying. I learned then that nothing is forever. I decided I would never again expect permanence, and I spent many years before Paul came on the scene training myself to live without depending on anyone else." She paused to take a sip of her drink. "Before I married Paul, I told him I would never allow myself to be dependent upon him. I thought it only fair to warn him there was a part of me I would keep in reserve. I felt I could never fully trust again."

Anthony looked stricken. "I had no idea it affected you that much. I guess all we could see was our own happiness together, and had no thought of what it must have done to you." He was silent for a moment, then leaned forward in his chair. "You never let on how you felt."

"What good would it have done? Spoiling your happiness just because mine was in tatters wouldn't have been worth it," she responded. "There isn't a whole lot of point in making more people miserable. And, ultimately, what difference does it make? It doesn't change what's happened." If only it had been as quick and easy as I'm making it sound, she thought.

Anthony got up to replenish his drink yet again. Scotch on the rocks. He returned to his easy chair and leaned back. They sat in silence.

"I guess you're right," he finally replied. "Thank you for that gift." He drank half the liquid down in one tip. "And you always shared the children with us, even though you didn't have to."

"I did it for them. They loved their father. Why should I try to poison them against him, and prevent them from having the benefit of that loving relationship?"

"Graham always appreciated it," Anthony replied, sinking further into his chair. "He always thought you were one of the greatest things ever to happen to him. He wished he could be what the straight world calls 'normal.' I was sometimes jealous of you. He held you in such high regard."

He finished his drink. "But the jealousy disappeared when you married Paul, and I didn't think of you as a serious rival anymore."

Molly laughed. "I can't imagine being considered a serious rival to anyone."

Anthony didn't laugh. "You were. Very much so." He looked into Molly's eyes. "You don't realize what you have. In spite of what you call your 'Rubenesque figure'—which has been seriously altered since Paul died—and what you think of as a plain face, you're really quite an attractive person. It's your eyes. Compassionate. Your concern for people radiates from you and makes people want to tell you their troubles. They feel you might hug them at any moment and take all their cares on your shoulders, and they'll be all right. You had that quality during university days. I think you became our 'earth mother.' We all loved you in our own ways. Both Graham and I hated losing you as our friend."

They sat in companionable silence for a while.

"The kids came to love you, too, Anthony," Molly said, breaking the silence. "You were always so good to them when they came. Taking them to Puerto Peñasco in Mexico...they told me all about digging a hole in the sand on the beach, putting a grate over it, and filling the hole with coals. And the old pot you filled with beer and sea water, and heated on the red coals to cook the giant shrimp you'd buy in the market. And the *limones*—those lemony lime citrus fruits you'd buy in Mexico. Squeezing the juice on the shrimp before eating them with your fingers. They loved those adventures.

"They also told me about the observatories on Kitt Peak, which enthralled them, and they became interested in desert plants and animals after you took them to the Desert Museum."

Anthony began squirming. He wasn't quite sure how to take all this praise.

"You expanded the children's horizons in many ways. I would never have taken them to places like the Pima Air Museum or the Titan Missile Museum. Even the girls enjoyed those outings and told me about them with enthusiasm. And you talked to them about philosophy and directed them to the many books you've read, titles and subjects they would never have delved into if I had suggested them."

The two sat with their own thoughts and memories.

"Anyway," Molly was again the first to surface, "you shared your home and your life and your intellect with them even though they weren't your kids."

"In their own way, Molly, they became my kids, the family I would never have. And like it or not, you have become the sister I never knew. I value your friendship above all. Thank you for being forgiving, and not abandoning us."

Anthony got up to make another drink. His speech was becoming slightly slurred, and Molly knew it wouldn't be long before he slid off to bed and passed out. She wondered if he had hangovers in the morning, and couldn't fathom how he could operate at all, with this daily assault of alcohol on his body and mind.

That night he became disgustingly drunk, and Molly reached the limit of her tolerance. The next day, a Saturday, she asked him if they could have a talk before he started drinking. He looked a little startled, but sat down with her.

"What's wrong, Molly?" he asked.

"You're killing yourself with alcohol, Anthony," she began. "I care about you and want to live here with you, but I can't do it anymore. I just can't bear to watch you commit suicide by drinking yourself to death." She took a deep breath and plunged on. "I'm sorry, but I'm going to move out at the end of the month. It's the only thing I can think of to do."

Anthony looked shocked. Then other expressions crossed his face, as he processed her comments. Neither spoke for several minutes, during which time Anthony's shoulder's slumped, and his facial expression turned to one of defeat. Molly saw tears forming in his eyes and felt like a mother abandoning her child, but forced herself to remain where she was, saying nothing.

Finally Anthony spoke, his voice thick. "Is there anything I can do to change your mind?"

"Yes," she replied, holding on to her resolve, "you can join AA."

"But I'm not an alcoholic," Anthony said indignantly, jumping up out of his chair. He seemed to tower over her as he stood, hostile, looking down. Then he started to pace the floor.

"Those of us who know you, and care about you, think you are," Molly said, sitting still, trying to remain calm and determined. "You're the only one who thinks you aren't."

She could tell Anthony was furious with her as he continued his pacing. Finally he stood before her again briefly to deliver his final question.

"Do you really think I care a damn what everybody thinks?" He left
the room without waiting for a reply. Molly didn't pursue him, and spent
the rest of the day in her wing practicing and studying as best she could.

That night Anthony drank even more than usual, and Molly retired
to her wing to avoid him. Supper sat in her throat like a huge lump. She
started packing her things and then, suddenly very tired, sank onto her
bed, wishing she hadn't come to Arizona.

* * *

About midnight, the doorbell rang. It woke Molly, who had managed
to fall asleep, much to her surprise. She didn't hear Anthony getting up
to answer, so she put on her dressing gown, went to the front door, and
looked through the peephole. No one was there. Had she dreamed the
bell, or had whoever was there left because it had taken her so long to get
to the door? If they'd left that soon, without ringing the bell again, it
mustn't have been an emergency. She decided to check the back yard in
case whoever it was had gone there to try to rouse them from their sleep.
She looked out and saw no one until her gaze moved to the pool. There
was something by the steps, half in the pool and half out. In the dim
light, it looked as if it might just be a bag, put there to lure her out of the
house to see what it was. And then what? She ran down to Anthony's
room to try to wake him and ask him what to do.

He wasn't there.

She raced back to the door, her heart beginning to pound. She
found the switch for the pool light and looked out. There was Anthony,
lying face down, with blood oozing from the back of his head. Had he
been fool enough to go for a swim alone, after drinking so much, and
fallen as he'd come out of the pool?

But the doorbell. It couldn't have been Anthony who rang the bell.
Dare she go out? Was there a burglar or, worse yet, a killer out there
somewhere?

Molly stood immobilized. Only six months ago she'd come home
to find her husband lying dead on the floor next to their front door.

Please, God, not Anthony, too. She became cold all over, her mind
and body frozen in horror.

After what seemed a long time but was really only a few seconds,
Molly's limbs and brain unlocked. Although she was afraid to venture
outside, she knew she must see if Anthony was still alive, and get help

for him if he was. She didn't know how long he might have been lying there because her wing of the house was away from the pool. Then she noticed the door out to the pool was already unlocked—of course, how else would Anthony get out, she chided herself—which meant that if a burglar was there, he could be inside the house already.

She might be safer outside than in.

Molly reached for the door handle, forcing herself to turn it slowly and quietly to ease the door open without making any noise. Then she realized how foolish she was being again—she'd already made enough noise to alert any burglar as to her whereabouts.

Once out, she went straight to Anthony, knelt, and took his arm to feel for a pulse.

It was there—weak, but regular.

Thank God.

She rushed back into the house to phone an ambulance and get a blanket. She was no longer worrying about culprits, in or out of the house.

Back at the pool, she tried to pull Anthony further out of the water, knowing she shouldn't move him, but not wanting him to die of shock or cold. She wished she'd taken a course on what to do in emergencies. Like most people, she just never expected them.

She covered Anthony and crouched beside him, talking all the while in case he could hear her. The ambulance drivers might think it a little strange to see him lying there without swim trunks, but she didn't care. Anthony always swam in the nude. "It's not a sexual thing," he'd told her. "It's comfort. Unless I'd be offending you."

After having a son and two daughters and being married twice, Molly was neither shocked nor surprised by the human body. She had assured Anthony he could be comfortable, and she wasn't going to try to put a bathing suit on him for the ambulance drivers. The blanket would have to do, whatever they thought.

It seemed to Molly it took forever for help to arrive, as she stayed by Anthony, making reassuring noises at him, afraid to touch him again in case she hurt him more, and praying he would survive. She had no thought of phoning the police. In fact, she wondered if she had imagined the doorbell ringing. Perhaps some angel of Anthony's had alerted her, making her wake up.

Later, as she waited in the hospital while Anthony was being admitted and looked after, she castigated herself for speaking to him about his drinking at all. She probably only made it worse.

Needing a "family fix," she phoned Peace River from the hospital. Her mother's response was, "Isn't it a good thing you're there with him."

"But it's all my fault," Molly moaned into the phone. "Bad things keep happening to people I care about. I must be jinxed." She tried to keep back tears.

"Nonsense," Ann told her. "Stop whining and don't be a fool, Molly. You're not responsible for anyone else's drinking. Instead of sniveling about being there, you might remember he was getting drunk long before you came and might have been alone when he hit his head and died because no one was there to help. He did it to himself. Don't allow yourself the luxury of feeling sorry for yourself. That's tiresome and selfish, and Anthony needs you to use your energy to help him instead."

"But I'd just told him I was moving out as soon as I could find a place."

"Good. That's tough love, just like you had to use on Shannon when she was a teenager. Keep in mind it was Anthony's choice to get drunk, and get your backbone in place again. I'll be down to help you soon. The weather here is getting too cold already. We've even had our first snow, and I'm ready to pack up and leave."

Ann's unsympathetic approach was actually very reassuring to Molly, who didn't want to be a whiner.

"You have a friend you can talk to there, haven't you? Phone that girl you used to know. Helene? Doesn't she live somewhere near you?" Ann asked.

"Not that near, Mom. She lives in Tucson. We're a half hour drive south of that. And she has problems of her own. I don't want to give her mine to worry about, too."

"You can commiserate with each other. Sometimes it helps put things into perspective if you talk them over with someone instead of holding everything inside. Your mind can quickly make a problem seem insurmountable if you think too much about it," Ann countered.

Molly did phone Helene when she got home after leaving Anthony at the hospital. Helene responded in much the same vein as Ann had, giving the same advice.

"Would it help if I came over?" Helene concluded.

"No...you have your own family to deal with. I'll be okay. But thanks for the offer. At least I know I can call on you if I need to. How are things at your place?"

"Georgia and I may be over to join you at Anthony's before you move out," Helene said, and abruptly hung up the phone.

* * *

When he regained consciousness, Anthony was unable to remember anything from the preceding twenty-four hours, including Molly's statement she was moving out. She told him again as he lay in the hospital bed with his head bound up. He looked stunned, and asked what he could do to make her stay. She gave him the ultimatum once more.

"It's because I care about you, Anthony. I can't bear to see you killing yourself. We've both had a lot happen to us this last year, and I'm sorry about your reasons for drinking, but I'm not dealing with any more trauma. That's what your excessive drinking is to me, and I can't take it. I'm not changing my mind about this, and I'm going out to look for a place this week," she reiterated.

"Give me this week, Molly. Please," Anthony begged. "Don't do anything until I have a chance to at least think about what you're saying. Please wait till I'm home from the hospital." He looked so woebegone she felt obligated to give him that time. At least he would be sober while he was in the hospital. However, that wasn't going to be very long, and she was sure the drying-out process, if he chose that direction, would be difficult.

* * *

Agatha had just about had it. The power-hungry maniac she'd once been foolish enough to marry was still here and busy wrecking her well ordered life. Why couldn't he just leave her alone? It had taken barely two years for him to completely demoralize her when they were married. She was lucky they'd divorced before she became a total basket case, unable to cope with the world at all.

Agatha had thought running away to get married would be an effective means of getting free from her father. She thought if she didn't escape, he'd find a way to keep her home so she couldn't marry anyone. If he'd ever discovered her clandestine romance, he'd have put an end to it immediately.

Agatha's father never allowed her to play her violin just because she enjoyed it. He was a failure as a musician, himself. A hack, determined his daughter would be the success he never was, with the only way he knew how to achieve that being to beat her into doing more and better work. Her practice could never be long enough or good enough for him.

But he was careful. He never hurt her in a way that would interfere with her playing. He just sent her younger brothers out to the yard to get a branch off one of the trees, just the size for whipping her legs until she practiced harder. Her brothers, jealous of all the attention her father gave her because she was going to be "the great musician," were glad to see her punished. Nobody would ever believe her father was that mean. If she told anyone, they'd only think her a hopeless neurotic. She'd never forgiven her mother for doing nothing to help her, leaving the disciplining of the children up to her father.

She'd often thought about killing her father. But, instead, she ran away to marry the first man who showed any interest in her.

Agatha's father cut her out of the family immediately. None of them would have anything to do with her. She'd disappointed them.

Agatha was proud she'd had the courage to leave one impossible situation, and disappointed she'd been stupid enough to end up with another abuser. She was nearly free of the second, though she still needed the small amount of money coming in monthly—all she'd extracted from her ex-husband at the time of the divorce. She hated taking anything from him, but she couldn't afford her studies without it. In two more years she'd have her degree and she'd never allow herself to be dependent on anyone again.

Why did he have to end up here, of all the places he could have gone? Well, she'd try to ignore him, pretend she didn't hear his insults and taunts. If this didn't work, she'd try something else to get him out of her life for good. She was stronger now. He wouldn't get the best of her this time. She'd show both her father and her ex-husband she was a survivor. She'd make it on her own.

* * *

Ruby was getting tired of being blackmailed. It was time to do something about it. All he wanted was for her to meet him at a motel one night every week for sex. And what was that to her, anyway? When she was married to him she learned what he wanted. It was one of the reasons they were no longer married. So what did it really matter?

What mattered was she was tired of being used. He wasn't going to destroy her again. Hell, she'd already been a hooker to get enough money for the drugs and alcohol she'd turned to in an attempt to survive his barbs, the wounding remarks that had cut her to bits. He'd thrown her out, the bastard! Disgraced her in front of everybody. And she'd gone to the bottom. He must have known she would. He knew how weak she was—after all, she fell for him, didn't she?

Soon after they were married, Ruby discovered all he wanted was a woman to destroy, bit by bit, in ways no one could even guess. By the time she realized what was happening, she was incapable of fighting back. She should have known he'd marry again. She should have warned his latest victim—but who ever believes a has-been, a former wife? Especially one in the state she'd sunk to by the time he cast her off. They would just consider her a jealous loser…someone he was well rid of.

Ruby managed to pull herself out of the pile of losers, by a miracle she still couldn't believe in, and he wasn't going to wreck it for her now. She'd sleep with him until she was ready to fix him for good. It didn't bother her anymore. And he'd keep quiet about it. No one would know what she'd been, now she was out of it. That was important to her here.

One of these days, soon, he'd know what it was like to be weak, cringing, dependent on someone else's mercy. It would be revenge for all the insults she'd endured. He'd be sorry they'd ever ended up in the same place. She'd let him think he could toy with her, and laugh at her, and use her. And then she'd strike. And she'd have the last laugh.

Ruby drove home to her new husband. She'd include him in her plan. He'd like that.

* * *

Anthony went to his first meeting of AA the night Molly brought him home from the hospital. He was still insisting he wasn't an alcoholic, but was willing to do anything to keep her from moving out. Molly wondered if, perhaps subconsciously, he knew he might drink himself to death if left with only his own thoughts to keep him company. Whatever the reason, he wasn't telling her.

After his first month of meetings, Anthony began talking about his AA experience as he and Molly had a wine-less supper.

"There's this Big Book, like an alcoholic's bible, written in 1935 by a number of men who were alcoholics. Some believe it was divinely inspired. Anyway, each meeting starts with a standard reading from the Big Book."

"What about women?" Molly asked, glomming on to the fact it was written by men.

"Women weren't included then, though they are now. I understand, though, that the wife of Bill W., the founder, used to gather the wives, and they made coffee and refreshments for the men's meetings. She and the others formed Al-Anon as a support group for family members of alcoholics, so she's pretty important to the program, too," Anthony replied. "At the meetings, after the reading, we get up one at a time, give only our first names, because anonymity is important to us, and say we're alcoholics. Then we talk about our problem with alcohol. Sometimes we tell how we came to AA. We have coffee and talk with one another. And that's it."

Molly looked at Anthony's Big Book when he left it on the coffee table, and read the chapter on 'wives of drunks.' Helene, who had a long acquaintance with the misuse of alcohol, had told her it was rather old-fashioned. Molly found it amusing, but realized, though the book was dated, it was still obviously useful, and that was what was important.

* * *

"What a treat not to be driving through snow in November," Molly said to Anthony. Now that he wasn't drinking and could be trusted to drive, Molly enjoyed being a passenger.

"That's one of the things I didn't miss when I left Edmonton," Anthony replied. He hadn't had a drink in thirty-five days, and they were off to the last AA meeting of the month, one to which family members or friends could be taken as guests. Molly felt honored Anthony had invited her to go with him. After each year of sober living, alcoholics speaking at the meeting would be those celebrating their AA birthday (as opposed to their chronological date of birth, which they called their "bellybutton birthday").

As they drove along, Molly asked Anthony why he was still going to a meeting every day. She couldn't imagine why anyone would voluntarily go to any meetings. She thought of those she'd had to attend when she was teaching—boring, fruitless meetings, at which someone was always trying to reinvent the wheel, speak educationese, and run sessions according to whatever formula was currently in vogue. The leaders predictably called themselves facilitators, and the agenda didn't usually have much to do with anything the teachers needed to settle at the meeting. They were practically always a complete waste of time.

"I have to go to a meeting every day," Anthony confided. "I need the group…the philosophy…my sponsor. I'm tempted to drink so often.

Without my daily meeting, I probably would have succumbed by now. 'One day at a time' is the best I can do, and that's the philosophy."

The only thing Molly didn't like about Anthony's transformation was having to forgo the glass of wine she always enjoyed with dinner, but it was a small price to pay so as not to tempt him. She felt mildly irritated by his allowing himself to get to the position of having to be all or nothing on alcohol, until she read a book explaining about alcoholism being a disease, and not something alcoholics did to themselves. A gene or something. It made sense…a physiological reason for some people drinking in an uncontrolled way, while others were not tempted.

Though pleased to be invited, Molly felt a little nervous about attending the open meeting with Anthony, not wanting to intrude on the privacy of the members of the group. Only people who were alcoholics, who could stand up and say so, were allowed at the regular meetings. She supposed those who wished to preserve their anonymity would not attend the open meetings, knowing visitors would be there.

Anthony had spent much of the first two weeks of his sobriety telling her, "I'm not an alcoholic, but I can't attend these meetings unless I say I am. Since you have threatened to move out unless I go, I say it."

Then he started telling her, "I say I'm an alcoholic at the meetings, because I know I need the group to help me quit drinking. But I'm not an alcoholic."

Near the end of his first dry month, Molly heard Anthony refuse a friend's offer to get him a drink, saying, "Drinking isn't good for me, and I've decided to quit. Do you have a soda?" Molly used to think he meant he wanted soda water, as he'd be served in Canada, before she learned people in many of the states referred to all soft drinks as sodas.

She was pleased when she heard him later, telling one of his colleagues, "I may be an alcoholic, so I've joined AA and am going to their meetings. Whether I'm an alcoholic or not, I know booze isn't good for me." He'd be over another big hurdle when he could say "I'm an alcoholic" to himself, as well as at his meetings.

As Molly looked at Anthony, she felt very much as if she were his proud big sister. Since he'd "got off the sauce," he looked about ten years younger. No longer was his the florid, flushed face of the chronic heavy drinker. He was beginning to lose weight, too, from the increased intensity of his morning and evening laps in the pool and the reduced intake of calories now he was no longer ingesting vast quantities of alcohol.

It was amazing. Such a change visible in so short a time.

Molly appreciated the advantages of a "dry" Anthony—not having to insist on being the driver when they went out in the evenings, not having to hold his arm so he wouldn't fall down the steps of houses after they'd visited his friends. Anthony had always been an interesting person, well read and knowledgeable about so many things. He was always asking questions wherever he went, learning from people in every walk of life. He hadn't lost his inquisitiveness, but now that he wasn't drinking, he didn't have the lapses of memory, the mini-blackouts that made him seem as if he were becoming senile. He wasn't constantly repeating statements and asking questions for which he had already received answers in the same conversation. She no longer had to remind him of conversations they'd had, appointments and promises made in the evening after he'd downed his first few drinks.

By the time they arrived, the meeting room was already very full. After briefly looking around, Anthony steered Molly to two chairs at the back of the room. Following readings from the Big Book, speakers began to take their turns at the podium.

"My name is Ruby, and I'm an artist and an alcoholic." Molly wondered if the first speaker lived in the arts community at Tubac, not far south of Green Valley, where the quality of the artists' work was generally high.

"I'm celebrating my first year of sobriety," she went on. "I never thought I'd make it and wouldn't have without the program." Though Ruby hadn't sounded or looked to Molly like someone who got emotional, she saw tears on her cheeks. They were quickly flicked away.

"It's given me a whole new way of life. Thanks to all of you, I've made it this far." She recovered herself quickly and seemed almost euphoric as she bounced away from the podium.

Molly looked at her carefully. She was sure she knew the woman from somewhere, but it wasn't from visiting Tubac. Tonight's encounter was out of context, and she just couldn't think where Ruby fit. She looked at the young, healthy woman, with her long face, full lips, and large, piercing blue eyes.

Molly filed Ruby in her personal "to remember later" file. The middle of the night was the fruitful time, when free-range thoughts seemed to pick up the crumbs of information her mind tried unsuccessfully to retrieve during the day. As she settled in to listen to the rest of the speakers, she noticed Anthony had crouched down lower in his chair beside her, as if hiding.

The next speaker appeared to be in his early fifties. He was tall and thin, and looked like an eccentric university professor, with his shock of white hair, carefully trimmed beard, and tweed jacket. When he began to speak, the image changed. "I'm Hal, and I'm an alcoholic. I got drunk only three times in my life. The first time, I beat up my wife and she left me. I never could get her back." He paused. "The second time, I got into a bar fight. My injuries were so bad I lost my leg. No way to get that back. The third time, I joined a bunch of barflies and robbed a store. Can't get a clean record back." He tugged at his beard, as if deciding how to go on. He seemed ill at ease being in the spotlight.

"In jail, I heard about AA. Figured drink was interfering with my life, which was all I had left," he continued, and looked around his audience. "So I joined, and this is my thirtieth birthday. I'm proud to be here. I have a job, a new wife and kids, and I'm a happy man, thanks to you guys." He gave a funny little wave and walked back to his chair, his prosthetic leg not obvious.

The next speaker looked like the quintessential little-old-lady librarian, except for the fact that she was wearing jeans and a t-shirt. Short and slight, she had white fluffy hair and wore glasses. Her pale face was without makeup.

"My name is Mabel, and I'm an alcoholic," she began with the ritual statement, "and my husband is here, too, but he'll speak for himself. He's been sober two days longer than me."

She paused and looked at her husband, who was beaming at her. "He calls them 'quality days' and claims he has vast spiritual superiority over me."

The group laughed appreciatively.

"I was a bar hopper and a fighter," she went on, grinning. "Fought with my fists. Always had broken arms or legs. My specialty was rotgut wine and the cheapest beer I could get. Spent a lot of time in jail. Met my husband, Bob, at a bar and we drank a lot together. The umpteenth time I landed in jail, I was also sent to a hospital.

"I was in the hospital when I decided I'd join AA as soon as I got out. So I did. Came home from one of the meetings and told Bob I didn't want any more alcohol in the house. So he joined, too." She surveyed the group before continuing.

"But then I blew it, went out, got drunk again, and had to start all over. And that's how he got the spiritual superiority."

The laughter was genuine and warm, and followed her as she returned to her chair next to Bob. Then he took his turn at the podium to confirm her story and tell his own. "And life has gotten better than I could ever have imagined in my wildest dreams."

The last speaker of the night was an eighty-five-year-old man who used his cane to help move his arthritic body slowly and painfully up to the microphone.

"I'm Leonard, and I'm an alcoholic. You're all anxious to get to that great looking cake and have some coffee, so I won't keep you from it for long." He adjusted the microphone for his height and continued. "When I sobered up, I discovered I hadn't paid income tax for twenty years. Now, you young folks all know that one of the things we do in AA is get right with our world. Make amends."

He paused, moved his cane slightly, "Well, I was indentured to the government for a mighty long time, but I've been a debt free and happy man for thirty years now, and sober for forty. I'm thankful I've had AA to help me get there." He looked around the room and, unlike many of the elderly, did stop there, saying, "Let's go have that cake."

The group applauded him and rose to get their cups of coffee and generous slices of birthday cake. They'd heard speakers identify themselves as a judge, a university professor, an accountant, an artist, a laborer, and a beautician, with from one to forty years of sobriety. A cross section of society.

The meeting was long enough for the smokers in the group to feel the need to make a beeline for the door to get outside for their nicotine fix. Molly was particularly sympathetic with the smokers' needs. Before she quit smoking, she remembered it was unthinkable to her to stop for a cup of coffee with a friend unless she had her cigarettes with her. She was relieved to be free of the addiction, but lived in fear she might start again if she ever took a cigarette. She called herself a "smokaholic," and was sure it was a true comparison, though some alcoholics wouldn't agree. She'd heard it was considered more difficult to quit smoking than drinking, and wouldn't be surprised if it were true.

"Listen, Molly, do you mind if we disappear quickly? There's someone here I'd just as soon not meet." Anthony took Molly's arm and steered her quickly to the door, away from a couple of women who seemed to want to waylay her.

As they hurried to the car, Molly asked, "Is it one of those women who were approaching me?"

"No. They're just friendly types who pounce on any visitor in case the person has come to join and could use some help," Anthony replied. "The belief is that it takes an alcoholic to help one. They like to make sure alcoholics get into the right hands."

"Who looks after these meetings?" Molly asked as they settled into the car and put on their seat belts.

"People take turns. If it's your turn, you make sure there's coffee, arrange for a speaker if it seems a good idea, and choose someone to read the page from the Big Book."

"When is it a good idea to have a guest speaker?"

"Today's group was much bigger than usual for this location, but with our small group, everyone has likely heard all the locals' stories a zillion times—though I haven't, being so new—so it's good to have an outsider speak to keep the regulars inspired."

"Always another alcoholic?" Molly asked as they drove out of the parking lot.

"Yes. Alcoholics helping other alcoholics who have the courage to change," Anthony replied as he drove onto the freeway.

Even though it sounded like a prepared statement, as if it had been memorized from a book of wise sayings about alcoholics, Molly was impressed. Anthony seemed to be getting closer and closer to admitting his affliction. She turned to look at him. "I guess I hadn't realized how difficult this would be for you."

"The meetings help," Anthony replied. "I'm told it's normal to go every day at the beginning. Ninety meetings in ninety days. And then another ninety meetings in the next ninety days, if that's necessary. I have a book that lists where to go in the general area so I can pick what's most convenient. There are so many, it's quite easy to slip into one wherever you are."

"I'm not sure I could manage meetings," said Molly. "They drive me batty."

"Listen, Molly, if alcohol is a problem in your life, AA is a way to solve the problem. It's not for everybody. You don't have the problem. Go ahead and have your glass of wine with dinner. I don't think it will bother me anymore...or if it does, I think I can handle it. I know you're trying to help me, but I know I want you back to normal."

"Helene was telling me people in Al-Anon claimed they didn't know anyone who was able to stay off the booze when the spouse continued to drink," Molly replied.

"You're not my spouse. No problem."

Did he speak from bravado? Should she believe him? For the rest of his life Anthony would be working and socializing with people who drank. Would he be able to stay dry in that environment?

Thinking it would be more difficult for Anthony when he was alone again, Molly decided at that moment to stay for the second term at the university, to give Anthony moral support and be sympathetic company for him until he was stronger.

As they neared the house, Molly remembered Anthony hadn't answered her question about why he wanted to leave the meeting.

"Whom were you trying to avoid tonight?" she asked.

Anthony's mouth set in a grim line, and he seemed lost in his own thoughts. He finally answered, inadequately, "Just someone who's been giving me trouble at the university. One of the problems that comes with the job. But someone I haven't seen at our meetings before and didn't know was in AA."

"Would it help to tell me about it?" Molly pressed him.

"No, I'm dealing with it. But I don't want any contact between my professional life and my AA right now. I'm going to have to avoid this group for awhile."

* * *

Ruby smiled to herself as she nibbled daintily on the cake and drank the scalding coffee. The sight of Anthony, who she knew was gay, and what she laughingly thought of as his "girlfriend" scurrying out of the hall like scared rabbits almost made her laugh out loud. Did the old fart really think she hadn't seen him skulking in the back row of the hall? What a silly man. You'd think his near death in the pool would make him wonder if someone was out to get him and think that maybe it hadn't really been an accident. He should have begun to feel vulnerable. Then, when he'd missed work because he was in the hospital, he should have changed his mind about the scholarships, but he was still being difficult about them.

Ruby decided she just had to persevere. Anthony was bound to weaken eventually and scare up some money for her. It wouldn't hurt to have extra ammunition to use to get him to do what she wanted. He wouldn't want everyone to know he was an alcoholic. God knows she'd been doing what everyone else wanted for too much of her life. No more. Now she was the user.

The really funny part of it was that people didn't even realize what she was doing to them. Anthony was as stupid as old Sneazewell. They weren't going to know what hit them by the time she was through.

Ruby was glad she'd chosen to attend the meeting in this location tonight. It was a good place for passing over the package she was to deliver to her husband's "friend." She knew she was a good actress and could make everyone think she belonged. The people in this group had all believed her sad little tale. It was that way at every meeting she attended. Anyone could pretend to be anything they wanted. What a joke it was.

Ruby turned to the young man who had sidled up to her. She recognized him as the person she was to meet.

"Would you walk me to my car? It's a little dark out there, and I don't like to go out unaccompanied." Ruby spoke loudly enough for anyone nearby to overhear her and think how nice it was of the young man to see her safely to her vehicle. The man nodded. She finished her coffee and they left.

Chapter 7

"You did pick up that God-damned score from the music stand after the rehearsal last night, didn't you?" Sneazewell roared into the phone. It was just before American Thanksgiving weekend, and his temper seemed to be reaching a peak.

"Of course. I always do," Agatha Holburn replied, adding under her breath, "asshole."

"I want the score for the Beethoven cleaned up right away and brought up to my office."

"What do you mean, cleaned up? Do you want me to rub out all your pencil markings and nasty remarks from the score and wipe the saliva off the edges of the pages?" Her hatred clouded her judgment, giving her the courage to be impertinent to this man even though he could make life so difficult for her.

"I want the low-level literacy removed, the slips of paper you left, which only remind me your intelligence barely reaches the two-digit mark," he said in an icy voice.

"I don't have the faintest notion what you're talking about. But then, that's no surprise," Agatha said.

"Don't play dumb with me, woman. Just get rid of them, and get the score up to me." He slammed the phone down.

"What's wrong with the great white leader this time, Agatha?" Trent Quillium, looking even more ungainly than usual, had come to the library to get a part missing from his music folder. Sneazewell's voice, too loud for the confines of a mere telephone, was unmistakable.

Who else would yell at Agatha? She seemed such a gentle person. Trent felt almost protective of her.

"That man is a boil on my life. He claims I've left notes in his score, and wants them cleaned up," she sighed, noticing that Trent was looking his usual woebegone self, his clothes unkempt and not very clean. She wished he would do something to make his appearance less of an affront to her sensibilities. Agatha was a fastidious woman who dressed well in spite of her limited resources. It didn't take a lot of money to stay clean, and at least he could trim his own hair to improve his appearance, she thought.

Agatha hunted through the music from the last rehearsal until she found the Beethoven score. "He thinks I'm stupid enough to waste my time writing notes to him in the score. As if I haven't better things to do. I suppose I'll have to look through the whole score just to try to find out what he's talking about. If I didn't need the money I get from this job to finish my degree, I'd quit."

Trent was concerned. He hadn't heard Agatha sound so negative before. He liked her, and hated the way Sneazewell treated her. He wished he had the courage to tell him off or do something to shut the man's mouth permanently.

He started to flip through the score, then stopped midway with a sudden gasp of laughter.

"What's so funny?" Agatha looked over his shoulder.

"There's a sticky note on page ten of the score."

Trent read the note aloud.

> "'Sneazewell's snotty suggestions
> Should be shoved right up his nose
> The hate we all have for him
> Daily grows and grows.'

"I like the signature, 'The G.R.O.S.S. (Get Rid of Sneazewell Soon) Society.' It's not really funny. It's just true. The verse isn't very good."

"I can see why he thinks I put it here. It reflects my sentiments exactly. And those of most of the other members of the orchestra, too. He must know how people feel about him." Agatha turned a few more pages of the score, carefully avoiding the discolored edges where Sneazewell's fingers had left their mark. "Here's another one," she said to Trent. "Listen to this:

'Sneazewell's silly tantrums,
Daily that he throws,
We'll show him lots of nasties,
With a heavy-duty hose.
                    G.R.O.S.S.'

"He's right about one thing, at least—the verses certainly aren't high literature. It sounds like someone's threatening him or trying to scare him."

"Lots of luck. Did you put them in his score?" Trent asked.

"Are you kidding?" Agatha said. "For one thing, I could certainly write better rhymes, and for another, I wouldn't dare threaten him." She continued leafing through the score. "This one is slightly better, verse-wise," and she read it to Trent.

"'Unsightly smelly Sneazewell
Go elsewhere for your play.
Don't take the chance of annoying us for
Yet another day.'

"And of course it's signed 'G.R.O.S.S.' That's clever. I like it."

"Too bad he didn't take the advice," Trent commented. "Why don't you play at being one of your namesake's detectives and find the person who wrote the notes?"

"Let me see that one," Agatha went on, ignoring Trent's suggestion. She took from his hand the piece of paper he had just removed from the score.

"'Such a sleazy Sneazewell,
Having lots of fun today
Badgering orchestra members
Who'll make sure you're sent away.'

"Signed 'G.R.O.S.S.,' again."

"Why is anyone wasting time like this? It sounds like a child. Surely the writer doesn't think this is ever going to help us get rid of the man. He's much too egotistical to think anyone could bring him down," Trent pointed out. "Here's another one.

'Oh, God, still here, old Sneazy?
Why do you dare come back?
What does it take to get rid of you?
A lethal good strong whack?'

"Whoever put these in must have figured Sneazewell wouldn't get through the symphony in one rehearsal, so this one was meant to be read the next time he rehearsed it. It shows whoever put them in must be in the orchestra, and knows he never gets through one piece, or even a movement, in a rehearsal and may want them to be discovered gradually. But who would be stupid enough to waste all this time, and chance getting caught?"

"I'd be frightened if they were written to me," Agatha said. "Listen to this:

'It's coming to you soon now.
If you look round everywhere
You will not ever see it.
You won't even know it's there.'

"I wonder if he's read this last one? He shouldn't treat it lightly."

"When you take the score up to him, why don't you suggest he show the notes to the police?" Trent asked.

"I don't usually remain in his presence any longer than I have to," Agatha sighed, picking up the score. "Stay and look after the place while I'm gone, will you, Trent?" she asked as she left the library.

Trent wandered around the room, looking at all the scores and parts that filled the shelves on every side of the room. He didn't know how Agatha could stand the job. Getting the bowings from the section principals was bad enough, but writing those bowings in all the string parts was mind numbing. She must really need the money. Trent sometimes helped her when she got behind in her work, especially on days he was anxious for company to try to pull himself away from sinking into deep depression. He'd do anything then. It was better to be marking bowings in the library than lying on his bed, alone in his room.

Agatha was taking longer than he expected, and he needed to go to the men's room. He decided it would be okay to leave the library for a few minutes.

When he returned, Trent found Ruby Reddick sitting at Agatha's desk with one of Sneazewell's scores open in front of her. She was screwing the top on her nail polish.

"Isn't this a rather odd place to paint your nails? Don't you have a home to go to?" Trent was annoyed at the familiar way in which Ruby had taken over Agatha's office.

"That's really not your business, is it, twerp? I know what I'm doing, but what are you doing here? Don't you have anyone to play with?" Ruby disliked Trent and made it very obvious every time they met. Trent usually tried to avoid her.

"I'm looking after the library while Agatha's running an errand."

"Not doing much of a job of it, are you? I could've stolen everything in the place."

"Oh, bugger off, Ruby. Agatha didn't say you were invited, and you're at her desk."

Ruby looked down at the desk and the score sitting there. Then she looked derisively at Trent. "Oh, dear," she sighed heavily, "how terrible of me. Have I usurped your few moments of importance?" Then she smiled sweetly and batted her eyes at him. She got up slowly and put the little bottle in her purse.

Trent thought at least she had the sense to know musicians don't wear gaudy bright nail polish. Hers was almost clear. In good taste. But that's about all the good taste he observed.

Ruby continued her baiting. "My poor bumpkin. I won't rain on your moment in the sun any more. Bye, bye, sweetie," and she swanned out the door, moving her hips provocatively, laughing as she went.

Trent followed Ruby out. "By the way, I hope you had a good time at the motel the other night. You and your illustrious companion," he said, not able to resist showing off to her, sick of her taunts. "I must ask Sneazewell if you're any good."

Ruby stopped, turned around, and gave him a look intended to reduce him to ashes. "I don't like people snooping around after me. Anything you think you might have seen involving my private life is none of your business. I would advise you not to irritate me, or you'll have to start watching your back. You never know what or who will be there," she said menacingly, and turned to stride aggressively down the deserted hallway.

The library was off in a corner of the basement of the music building, isolated from most of the student traffic when there wasn't an orchestra rehearsal. Trent wondered what the real purpose of Ruby's visit had been, and if she had accomplished it while he was in the men's room. Her warning made him uneasy. He thought her an evil person and perfectly capable of hurting him. But not if he acted first. He sat in the chair she had vacated and picked up the score she'd been looking at when he returned to the office. What could it tell him? Berlioz. *Roman Carnival.* Viola solo. He flipped through the pages. No notes. So that wasn't it.

"What's up? I just met Ruby on the stairs, and she glared at me and swooped by without even a greeting," Agatha said when she returned.

"I don't know. We certainly weren't having a coffee klatch. She is a right bitch. Do you always lock the door when you run errands?" Trent asked.

"I try to remember to. Not when I go to the washroom, but if I'm leaving the floor I do. Why? What did Ruby want?"

"Good question. But she was looking at this score of the Berlioz when I returned from the john."

"Well, it couldn't be important, or she would have said something when she saw me. Did she leave any notes in it?" Agatha sat at her desk and leafed through the score.

"No," Trent said. "That was the first thing I checked after she left."

"Do you have the time or inclination to mark some bowings for me?" Agatha put the score away and hauled out her work. "I'm getting behind again."

"I hate it, but for you I will."

They worked for an hour without interruption. Then Trent suddenly erupted, "Why do we take such crap from Sneazewell? Why do any of us? Why don't we just tell him to eff off?"

Agatha eyed him with alarm. He was usually so mild-mannered. Sneazewell's nastiness must really be getting to him, too, if he cared as much as his outburst implied. "Everyone has a reason. Each reason is different. Sneazewell knows how to get to us. He attacks us when and where we're vulnerable, where he knows we can't get back at him, where we're afraid. He is the lowest of the low."

"I'm surprised he's lasted here this long."

"With any luck, he won't be here much longer."

"What do you mean by that?" Trent asked.

"Oh, maybe he'll move along. I don't know. Let's talk about something more cheerful."

"Like your bass-playing friend, Andrew Penwith? I've seen him hanging around the library a lot."

"He used to visit once in a while, but he gave it up. He's just a nerd who thinks he knows more than the principal bass. He was playing a sneaky little game, but I got on to him fast. He thought he could put better bowings into the bass part than the principal bass did, and no one would notice his changes. So he came in here claiming to want to help bow the parts. I think he got the idea from seeing you helping sometimes. He thought I would be too stupid to catch on to what he was doing." Agatha laughed. "Then he wondered why I always had the bass parts done when he dropped by."

"He talked to me last week after he'd been in here with you and Jolene. He sounded as if he wanted to get to know the two of you better."

"Tough. If that's the case, he hasn't chosen the right method to go about it. And anyway, Jolene is married, poor woman—you know who her husband is—and I'm not interested. Anyway, he's a child."

"I don't know who Jolene is married to," Trent said. "I never know what the gossip is, and I never get to know the people in the orchestra. It's just too difficult trying to talk to them."

"You don't really try, that's why. You're not curious enough about other people, or you'd learn how to ask them questions. Most people like to talk about themselves," Agatha said, trying to give him some motherly advice. "And Jolene is married to old Sneazewell. I thought everyone knew."

"But...you and Jolene are friends," Trent said, surprised.

"In a way we are." Agatha returned to her marking without further comment, effectively cutting off the conversation.

Trent returned to his job, wondering about Jolene's marriage to the conductor who never even acknowledged he knew her. And what had Agatha meant by her suggestion that Sneazewell might not be there much longer? Did she know more about the notes than she let on? Was she in cahoots with someone else to frighten him into leaving? If that was so, he wished them luck.

Trent found these women hard to understand. One minute they could be so friendly, and the next they were biting off his head. He never knew what to say to keep them happy; that is, when he found the courage to talk to them at all.

Chapter 8

Molly's mother returned in late November, a little early for the Christmas holiday, but welcomed nevertheless. Ann was enjoying not having to don fur-lined boots and a heavy winter coat every time she wanted to venture outside. Fall had been particularly frigid in Edmonton and Peace River. It had not warmed up enough to melt the heavy snowfall they had suffered in early November. Ann had been glad to say good-bye to her apartment and friends in the seniors' housing complex and her other children in Peace River as she left to join Molly and Anthony in the warm Arizona sun.

In early December, with classes, orchestra rehearsals, and concerts in full swing, the term nearly over, they were sitting with coffee after dinner when Anthony said, "I have a favor to ask of you."

"After beef stroganoff and egg noodles al dente, the way I prefer them, and that delicious tossed salad, you can ask anything of us," Molly rashly replied, leaning back in her chair and folding her hands over her well-filled stomach. She was gaining back some of the weight she lost, thanks to Anthony's culinary prowess.

"Yes," Ann echoed, "as long as it doesn't involve moving too far or too fast. All this wonderful eating is exhausting me."

"Will you come with me to a chamber music concert tomorrow night in Tucson?"

"That's easy," Molly replied. "Mom, you want to come, too, whether you know it or not."

"Don't boss me, dear. If I come at all, it will be for Anthony the cook, not the chamber music and not a bossy daughter."

"It will be a good concert," Anthony continued. "The stickler is its dedication to Graham. No one knows you were Graham's wife, Molly, so that's not a problem. I've been cornered into this by a cello student of his who seems to have had a mad crush on him, and who, I'm afraid, is transferring all this irritating attention to me." He looked tired and pained. "I don't know if this is all that appropriate," he went on, "but the members of the quartet have agreed, and it gets Trent Quillium off my back."

"Honestly, it doesn't bother me, Anthony," Molly assured him. "Don't fret. We'll be happy to come."

As they drove into the city the next evening, Anthony described the musicians they would be listening to.

"Molly, you know most of them from your orchestra rehearsals."

"I don't know many of the orchestra members yet, Anthony. I get there just in time for rehearsal and rush away to get home in time for supper. Anyway, bass players are stuck off in the corner together and take so long getting packed up and put away that everyone else has escaped before they're ready to leave. So tell us all about them. Maybe I'll recognize them when I get there."

"Marguerite Larkowach is the first violinist. She's not a great musical talent, but she's very bright and a hard worker. Totally reliable. She's the woman with the long black hair and dark intense eyes. She was in my office when you came by yesterday. Takes herself a little too seriously, very stolid and sturdy about everything, but reliable. A pity she's the first violinist, though. Her vibrato is a little too fast and nervous sounding to allow for a beautiful tone."

"You mean the kind of nanny goat vibrato that starts immediately and stays the same speed right through the note?" Molly asked.

"Right. Doesn't ever get into the notes expressively. A little mechanical."

"I thought you said this was going to be a good quartet. It doesn't sound like it," Molly ventured.

"Oh, she's not quite as bad as I make her out to be. I just find her irritating. She's the kind who follows every musical rule carefully and accurately, but totally without spontaneity. That's why she'll never be great no matter how well she plays in tune or how accurate her rhythm. There's no sparkle, no taking chances, no personality."

"Is this how you speak to your students when you're encouraging them to attend a performance?" Ann asked pointedly.

"Sorry, Ann," Anthony apologized. "It'll be good. I just had enough of her whining yesterday about some little detail not included in the program. She wants it specially announced. She's so afraid she won't get full credit for everything she's done since she was born." He sounded peeved.

"The second violinist is an off-the-wall character. Leon Henwood. He can barely sit still, he's so hyperactive. But he's fun to talk to and to be around. He's the kind of person who finds excitement in the mundane and shares it with you. He's probably the one who puts the life into the quartet, while still managing to subdue his individuality sufficiently to match the sound of the other members of the group."

"He sounds like fun," Molly said enthusiastically. She enjoyed her own rascally students, even though they were far more trouble than the well-behaved ones.

"He is." Anthony went on. "Then there's Joan Laird on the viola. Nice girl. Very expressive playing, with a warm, rich, full tone. And the cellist is Walter Laskin, the weak link. His playing is very expressive, but he's not always fastidious about his rhythm. Not bad, mind you, just not perfect. Which means the group is always a little nervous about him, of course."

"I know most of those names," Molly told him. "Several of them are people Sneazewell picks on in orchestra. Walter's the cellist he goes on at about rhythm, but he's nasty to just about anyone who isn't a principal player. And he's positively vicious to poor Trent Quillium."

"Sneazewell is an offensive little man, but he's rarely wrong about musicians."

"I'm not questioning his judgment, just how he deals with them. He's a tyrant."

They arrived at the concert venue in good time. It was one of those wonderful old churches built before the cost was prohibitive, with stained-glass windows and natural hardwood. It was equipped with a pipe organ, instead of one of the more modern electric organs Molly loathed. Even though they were not going to hear the instrument at the concert, she still liked the idea of being in a church with what she called a "real" organ.

Accompanied by Molly and Ann, Anthony went backstage briefly to wish the performers well. He introduced them to Joan Laird, the viola player, whom Molly recognized from the orchestra and had met previously through Helene. Anthony left them with her, and went off to greet the others.

Molly thought Joan quite beautiful. She had an English type of peaches-and-cream complexion, expressive eyes, and a wonderfully wide, toothy smile. Joan greeted them warmly and introduced them to the young man with whom she'd been chatting before they arrived. Sturdy in build, with dark hair and a strong clean-shaven face, her companion seemed reluctant to take his eyes off Joan. When he turned, dragging his attention away from her, he and Molly recognized one another from their classes and orchestra rehearsals.

"Hello, Richard." Molly greeted him warmly and introduced her mother.

"Of course, you know our guest performer from the orchestra." Joan Laird looked at Molly as she spoke. "He's doing the bass part with us tonight when we perform the *Trout Quintet* in the second half." She turned to Ann. "But don't try to talk to him about bass. He just talks about trains, and then you can't get him stopped." Joan's bright, warm smile made this a proud statement rather than a criticism.

Anthony came up to them at that moment. "Richard, I'm glad to see you. These are my Canadian friends, Molly and Ann O'Connor."

Richard's face lit up immediately. "Here we've been playing together in the orchestra all this time, and I didn't know you were from Canada. Have you ever done the train trip through the Rocky Mountains? I can hardly wait till I have the time and money to go to Calgary and Banff to ride that train to Vancouver."

Molly laughed at his enthusiasm. "I did the trip years ago, and it is good. Especially the mountain part."

"Richard's life revolves around trains. He has model trains, contributes articles to train magazines, and has connections all over the world with his Internet activity." Joan Laird looked fondly at her friend. Molly wondered why she hadn't noticed they were a pair before, but, as she'd told Anthony, she hadn't had much time to meet people other than Helene at the orchestra. She'd been so busy trying to hone her bass skills to keep up with these young kids, she'd barely had the energy to think about people and relationships.

After their brief chat with the players, Anthony and the two women made their way to the main body of the church, leaving the quartet to their tuning and warming up.

The church was half full, a good audience for a midweek concert so close to end-of-term exams. Anthony spied a student who had registered for bass as an option and would be playing in the orchestra with Molly in the second term.

"Kalid, come and meet Molly." Anthony drew the young black man into his sphere. "Molly, this is Kalid Jones, who is presently in journalism but plans to go into law. Kalid, Molly is another queer duck. She's a Canadian, but we don't hold that against her." They all laughed. "You and Molly will be in the orchestra together next term."

"And why is Anthony calling me 'another queer duck'?" Molly asked Kalid as she shook hands with him.

"I'm the other queer duck. They think I'm a little off, because I'm in the military reserve as well," Kalid replied with a twinkle in his eyes. "Some musicians and academic types have this prejudice about the military—they don't think it's possible to combine them. But we won't bore you with that now."

"He's smart as a whip and a very fine bass player as well, so we don't hold his extracurricular involvement against him. He'll be the only non-music-major in the orchestra next term and can play circles around most of the others," Anthony explained.

"Don't believe everything you hear," Kalid told her, and turned his attention to Ann. "But do introduce me to this beautiful woman."

Molly introduced her mother. She could tell Ann was quite taken with this man with the liquid eyes and the facile tongue, who had the most enormous hands Molly had ever seen. She could imagine those hands caressing the double bass as if it were a delicate little instrument, and looked forward to hearing him play.

They chatted for a few more minutes and then found seats together near the back, a little apart from the rest of the audience, which had bunched up near the front. The church had been chosen because its acoustics were good wherever you sat, and because it was administered by a vestry and minister who were sympathetic to good music and didn't charge the students for its use.

"Have you seen Trent Quillium yet?" Anthony asked Kalid. "He was particularly interested in this concert and its dedication, and I don't see him anywhere." He sounded a little annoyed. "He'd better get here, after I've gone to the trouble of trying to please him."

"No, but I just arrived. Richard and Joan asked me to come along to hear their *Trout* and comment on it," Kalid replied.

The performers were coming on stage and conversations ceased. Marguerite announced that the performance of the Fauré quartet was dedicated to the memory of Graham Winslow, and they began.

Molly was soon aware she wouldn't have to worry about these performers. Their intonation was secure. They sounded like reliable musicians. She could relax and listen for ensemble playing and the matching of tone qualities. Anthony, she thought, had been too critical. Maybe he was put off by the "swing and sway" movement some members adopted. It was very distracting and didn't seem to have much to do with the direction of the bow or the emotional content of the music. Molly wondered if they bobbed around because they thought it made them look more musical. She found she enjoyed the music more if she just closed her eyes and let it float over her.

Halfway through the first movement, an untidy young man came noisily in the back door of the church. He lurched down the aisle, stopping at the front pew, where people were forced to stand up to let him through as he pushed his way to the middle of the row.

"That's disgusting. What is that man doing coming in while the musicians are playing? If he doesn't know enough not to interrupt, why is he here?" Ann hissed at Molly. "Someone should speak firmly with him."

"Don't be a snob, Mother. You're interrupting just as much by complaining about him. It's one of the bass players in the orchestra, and he does know better. I don't know why he's come in late. Now let's shush," she whispered back.

Ann shot Molly one of her "Don't speak to your mother like that" looks, elevated her nose, and, having the last word, said, "At least that chap with the braid who came in after him managed to avoid any attention." Molly shook her head, wondering why her mother noticed so much more of what was going on around her than she did. She suspected her mother barely listened to the music and was more interested in the people surrounding her. She closed her eyes again and allowed herself to drift off into la-la land, where she liked to be while listening to music.

Ann leaned over after they had clapped their appreciation at the end of the Fauré. "Did you notice how expressive the cellist's movements were?"

"I think you like him just because he looks like your grandson," Molly replied grumpily. "Frankly, looking at these performers drives me mad. I had to close my eyes so their body movements didn't distract me from the music, or make me seasick."

"That bloody Trent Quillium, for God's sake." Anthony was furious. "He's missed the piece he insisted we dedicate to Graham. And what about that bass player of yours?" he turned to Molly accusingly.

"Andrew Penwith, Anthony," Molly supplied the name. "And I resent you calling him one of mine just because we both play the bass."

"Yours or not, he's eccentric, but I've not seen him drunk at a performance before. At least, I assume that's why he made that appalling entrance."

Just as the musicians were taking their last bows, there was another disturbance. A tall, gangly young man, dressed completely in black, staggered noisily from the back of the church, stumbling and shuffling his way down the aisle. When he arrived at the first pew he stopped, looking up at the musicians with a bewildered expression on his face. Then he lurched forward to the performers' chairs and collapsed at their feet.

"People have rather strange concert manners in Tucson, Anthony. What on earth is that boy doing here? He looks drunk and unkempt. I don't believe this is in very good taste." Ann sounded sententious.

The members of the audience had stopped clapping and were murmuring to each other, puzzled by this latest interruption. The musicians were clutching their instruments and staring at Trent Quillium's recumbent form. The first violinist, Marguerite Larkowach, pulled her foot out from under him and screamed, "There's blood on me!" The other musicians, holding their instruments protectively to the side, kneeled to examine Trent.

Joan Laird exclaimed, "He's bleeding. Somebody get an ambulance."

Molly remembered seeing a phone where the musicians had warmed up in the choir room at the side of the church.

"You stay here, Anthony," she said, poking him. He seemed to be in some kind of shocked state. "I'll go and call for an ambulance, and the police while I'm at it," she finished as she moved out of the pew. She didn't know if there had been what is called "foul play" in the old detective stories she'd read, but she had attended enough performances to know it wasn't the usual encore.

The musicians who were not playing in the Fauré were in the choir room wondering what the commotion was about, and why the quartet hadn't come off stage when the clapping stopped. They clustered around Molly to find out what was going on.

After Molly explained, they all went to the sanctuary of the church, where members of the quartet were still hovering over Trent. They were now surrounded by members of the audience who wanted a closer look at the victim.

No one seemed to know what to do.

"Like a bunch of vultures," Ann remarked, having remained in her own pew. "Do stay here with me, Molly. It can't be good for the young man to be surrounded by all those people. Anyway, it's not good manners to stare at someone in trouble."

When she heard the ambulance sirens, Molly left her mother to usher the attendants inside. They pushed their way through the crowd of onlookers and demanded room to examine Trent.

"This man's been stabbed," one of the attendants said, and looked around at the people nearby. "Move away, go sit down, but don't leave. The police will want to talk to all of you." They began looking after Trent's immediate needs. The police arrived and conferred with the ambulance personnel as they were loading Trent onto a stretcher to take him away.

Audience members, shocked, had gone to the pews as instructed. Molly noticed a few, including Andrew Penwith and the man with the braid Ann had seen, sidling to the side door and leaving quietly. She wondered why they left, and didn't know if she should run after them or point out their departure to the police. She decided to wait and see if there was any reason to mention it.

The police turned their attention to the audience and performers remaining, questioning them and taking their names and addresses before sending them home. Anthony and the two women stayed, along with the musicians who knew Trent Quillium personally, to tell the police what they had seen and what they knew about him.

Richard, the bass player, and Ruby Reddick, who was in the choir room with him, were asked to stay to answer questions as well. Molly and Ann had not been introduced to Ruby before. She looked familiar, though. Suddenly Molly was able to place her.

"Are you a violinist in Sneazewell's orchestra?" Molly asked.

"Yes," Ruby replied, and turned away from Molly, cutting her off. Molly shrugged and returned to her seat, wondering why the woman had been in the choir room at all if she wasn't performing.

Those required to wait for the police to get around to questioning them sat disconsolately in the hard pews. Anthony finally asked if he could take Molly and her mother home. This was one time when Ann should have been happy to take advantage of her age, but she seemed more annoyed than relieved when Anthony ushered them off to his car. It was nearly midnight by the time they got home.

When they opened the door, exhausted, the scene before them was almost too much to bear after what had already happened. Everything was in confusion. The house had been broken into and ransacked while they were gone. Ann and Molly stood still, stunned, not quite able to take in what they saw. Anthony called the police.

By the time the fingerprint routine had been done, leaving an even greater mess, and the police had asked all their questions, the trio was beyond exhaustion and completely depressed. Still, they had to straighten things up enough to go to bed. They started with Ann's room, worried about the effect of all this on a person her age. She even accepted being tucked in first, her fatigue making her grateful for their attentions.

Molly and Anthony sorted papers, remade beds, swept up broken crockery, and vacuumed up soil from tossed plants. They didn't have the energy to talk and worked silently, their minds in turmoil.

When they had finally finished, Molly voiced her thoughts. "Do you suppose tonight's break-in and the attack on Trent are connected in any way?"

"Who knows?" Anthony replied. "But how could they be? Aach...I'm too tired to even consider it."

By the time they made it to bed, it was nearly time to get up again.

As Molly dropped off to sleep, she had a vision of where she'd seen Ruby Reddick apart from orchestra. Oddly enough, it was with Sneazewell; the two of them were going into a motel. She'd taken a wrong turn on her way home one night and found herself in a part of the city she didn't usually go through. She'd thought nothing of it at the time. Then another picture entered her mind, of the same young woman weeping with joy at the AA open meeting she'd attended with Anthony. What had triggered these memories? Oh, who cares, Molly thought. What matters more is poor Trent Quillium. What hospital had he been taken to? Is he recovering? Is he even still alive?

Molly didn't know anyone she could phone in the morning to find the answers to her questions. Anthony was no help. He had no contact with the law and didn't seem inclined to pursue any inquiries. She hated being in a strange place where she had no contacts. She felt so vulnerable. She wondered if she had put her mother in danger by encouraging her to visit Arizona again.

Sleep finally came, in spite of her questions.

Chapter 9

The rude sound of the phone woke Molly the next morning, at an hour she did not consider part of a civilized person's day.

"Molly, I need you—now." Helene sounded almost hysterical.

"Of course. Where are you?" Molly was instantly caught up in the tension, her heart tightening in fear for her friend.

"Georgia and I are in Nogales. Stateside of the border. In a motel. Hiding. Don't suggest we come to you in a taxi. Edwin could trace it. We're registered under the name of Fielding."

"I'll come right away." Molly got the name of the motel, room number, and directions and hung up. She threw on a sweat suit, grabbed her keys, and ran out the door. As she passed Ann's room, she saw her mother was awake, cautioned her not to open the door to anyone she didn't know, and told her where she was going. As she backed her car out of the driveway, she saw Anthony had already left for work, and then began to worry about Helene missing an important exam scheduled for that morning. Things must be really bad if she was jeopardizing her term, and that meant it must be about Georgia, whose welfare was currently the only thing more important to Helene than her university studies.

Once she was on the highway driving south, Molly's brain seethed with questions. Obviously, the problem was with Georgia and Edwin. Helene said Georgia was with her, so that was good. Georgia was safe. Her mind began making jumps from one possible scenario to another. Had she uncovered Edwin's actions? Was he after Georgia? Had he been successful? He must be the problem, or Helene wouldn't be hiding from him.

As Molly sped along the freeway, past Tubac and the newest upscale golf course, she began getting fanciful in her imaginings, making connections where none could possibly be. Had Helene's problems with Edwin anything to do with the attack on Trent Quillium the previous night, or the trashing of Anthony's house? She couldn't see how, but people in the music department were far too involved in this spate of difficulties for them not to be connected in some bizarre way. She thought of Anthony's injury in the pool. Perhaps it wasn't an accident, after all. Did it have something to do with the break-in? None of it made sense to her.

She decided to try to put the blizzard of thoughts out of her mind until she'd dealt with Helene's problems, and turned on the radio to try to distract herself from her thoughts. She was able to find the motel easily, and parked the car in front of the number Helene had given her. She ran to the door and knocked lightly.

"It's Molly." She saw the curtain twitch at the window, then heard furniture being moved and a rattle as the safety chain was undone. Helene and Georgia looked haggard, as if they'd been under siege. Their faces quickly revealed their relief at seeing her, but their appearance shocked Molly.

"Did anyone follow you?" Helene asked, grabbing her, pulling her into the room, and shutting the door quickly.

"Not that I noticed," Molly replied. "I didn't even consider the possibility. I'm sorry."

"Let's hurry, then."

Gathering their few possessions, they dashed frantically to the car, urging Molly to drive away quickly as Helene and Georgia crouched down in the back seat. Molly, catching the heightened tension, nervously maneuvered the car out of the parking lot and onto the freeway, looking in the rearview mirrors, expecting at any moment to see someone following.

"Can't we go faster?" Georgia asked in a high-pitched voice.

"Not unless you want us to be stopped for speeding," Molly replied. "But from the look and the sound of the two of you, it would be a good idea to have some contact with the police."

"NO," they both yelled in unison.

"All right, you obviously don't want to be seen, so just stay down and I'll drive carefully. We're not far, so it won't be long." Molly concentrated on her driving while the two frightened women kept out of sight. Though Molly was anxious to hear what had happened, she managed to keep herself from grilling the two. They remained hidden for the rest of the drive, and no one spoke as they sped along the freeway.

When they got to Anthony's, they hustled out of the car and into the house almost furtively. Helene locked the front door and checked the other doors. Ann appeared from the bedroom wing to greet them and led them into the kitchen, where she had already started coffee.

Molly took juice from the refrigerator. "Sit down and tell us what's happened. Coffee's ready, but you look as if you need some proper nourishment first. I'll make some toast. Drink this now while your coffee cools."

Georgia and Helene poured themselves juice and drank thirstily. Ann brought a jug of milk and another glass for Georgia. Molly slid two pieces of whole wheat bread into the toaster while Ann set the table for breakfast. Their two guests huddled together at the table like two refugees just rescued from a boat drifting in the sea. Ann fussed around them, making sure their juice glasses were refilled, buttering their pieces of toast, laying out the jams and marmalade, mothering them as she waited for them to recover some semblance of normalcy. Georgia was shaking, and Helene was sticking close, giving her little hugs, rubbing her back, patting her hand.

When they finished their breakfast, Molly could contain her curiosity no longer.

"Give," she demanded, sitting down across from them with her own cup of coffee.

"Don't terrorize the girls, Molly," Ann admonished her daughter. "You can see they've had enough. Let them tell us in their own time."

"Sorry, but I can't stand it. Mom can be the polite hostess. I need to know what's happened."

Helene drained her coffee cup and gave Georgia another hug before responding. "After we talked in the cafeteria, I began watching Edwin very carefully—especially how he behaved when Georgia was around. And I started noticing little things. I started going home at times when he thought I'd be at rehearsals, which he knows I never miss. Edwin was always surprised to see me, scurrying around when I came in unexpectedly, being unusually solicitous."

"I wondered why you were leaving so early a couple of times without saying anything to me, but didn't want to ask," Molly said.

Helene paused and looked sheepish. "He'd put this smarmy smile on his face when I came in the door—the same smile I used to think was quite charming. The smile I took to mean he loved me madly. I'm such a fool."

They all sat still, waiting for Helene to continue her story. When she began again, her voice was strong and angry. "Every time I came home, if Georgia was there, she'd be in her room with the door locked. When she came out for meals, I noticed she wouldn't even walk near him, avoided being in the same room. And then I noticed how she inched her chair further away from him at the dinner table all the time. Most days, she didn't even come home until my scheduled return, or I'd have to phone her friends to find out where she was." She turned to Georgia and said, "If I'd known what he was doing, I would never have let it go on like this."

Georgia wept. "I know that now, Mom. But…you were so happy at the university, I didn't want to spoil it for you. I thought you loved him and would only believe him."

Ann gave Georgia her handkerchief, and Georgia dabbed at her eyes. She looked back at her mother. "He said you'd never believe me if I told you. He kept saying it was 'our little secret,' and…oh, he frightened me with his stories of how awful it would be if I told you."

"How could I not have seen what was going on? I'll never forgive myself," Helene said, and took Georgia's head in her hands. They were oblivious to anyone else.

"Remember this, always," Helene said as she looked into Georgia's eyes. "You are my baby, and I will always love you and believe you. No one else will be more important to me, ever…ever…ever. And I will keep telling you this until you are sick of hearing it."

Helene then embraced her daughter and rocked her back and forth, crooning as a mother does to her baby. Molly and Ann sat quietly, not disturbing them.

After awhile, they sat back in their chairs and wiped their eyes. Then, noticing Ann and Molly again, Helene said, "Sorry—we get a little carried away. But I discovered that bastard was trying to get into her bed."

Georgia looked embarrassed, but Helene forged on. "That's why she got the lock. Apparently this began not long after we got here, only now he's starting to terrorize her instead of using his 'friendly' approach. The creep."

Helene glared at Molly as if she were Edwin. "And when she locked him out of her room and kept out of his reach, he told her she'd better start thinking about being more 'friendly' or he'd tell me she was leading him on, and had been since we married. But only when I wasn't home, of course. I can't believe the low-life would do this to us. Yesterday I came home and found him trying to break into her room. Georgia was making so much noise screaming at him to get away from her, he didn't hear me come in. I was so angry I hit him with the nearest thing I could pick up. He fell. Luckily, it just knocked him unconscious."

"I wish he was dead," Georgia hissed.

"Understandable," Ann said, reaching across to pat Georgia's hand.

"I do, too. I just don't want to go to prison for doing it." Helene was emphatic.

"Go on," Molly said.

"While he was unconscious, I calmed Georgia down enough to unlock the door. We grabbed some personal stuff and our purses and got out of there as fast as we could."

"How do you know he's not dead?" Ann asked in her forthright way, though frightened of what the answer might be.

"He must have come to just as we were leaving, because he came staggering out of the house as we were backing his car out of the driveway. He started ranting at us, running after us. As we drove away, we could hear him screaming he'd have us charged for stealing his car and attacking him in his own home. He looked like a maniac, he was so enraged."

"If he's not dead, I hope he's hurt bad," Georgia said. "He told me I'd better not make him angry or he'd make sure Mom was never allowed on the university grounds again. He said she'd hate me for ruining things for her. He told me her classes were the most important thing in her life, and I'm ashamed to say I believed him." Georgia's face was blotched and her nose stuffed up from all the crying, but she seemed to be gaining confidence.

"As if classes could be as important to me as my own child," Helene said indignantly, tightening her arm around Georgia. "He must think I'm as much of a monster as he is."

"Where did you leave his car?" Molly asked.

"We drove down to the shopping center, the Wal-Mart one, parked it, and got a cab from there to the motel. We locked his car keys in the trunk before we phoned the cab."

"I didn't think to wipe our prints off the car," Georgia added, recovering enough to reach for another piece of toast. "He probably phoned the police and said we stole it."

"Ugh. As if we would keep anything of his. We don't want anything that man has touched. We just want him gone." Helene shuddered.

"Well, you've come to the right place to get away from him. You know you can stay here. There's plenty of room, and I know Anthony will welcome you," Molly told them.

"You two look as though you could use a nice hot shower and a good rest," Ann said. "Come with me and we'll get you settled into your room. There's one just down this hall, especially for you. There'll be time enough after you rest to decide what happens next."

Helene and Georgia hugged Molly and followed Ann, who gave them Molly's extra nightgowns to wear while she washed and dried their clothes.

When they were settled, Molly announced she was going to the university and would be home in a few hours.

* * *

Molly surprised Anthony at his office in the music building.

"You're up early."

"I am. What do you know about Edwin Hanson?" Molly asked without preamble.

"I've been on committees with him, and quite frankly, I thoroughly dislike him," Anthony answered. He explained he had never suggested Molly invite Helene over for a visit because he was afraid she'd have to bring Edwin, and he refused to have the man in his house. Molly had fleetingly wondered why this big sociable animal had never suggested a get-together with Helene and her husband, but hadn't brought it up. He was already looking after her mother, an extra guest he hadn't counted on when he invited Molly down.

"It's funny you should ask me that just now," he said. "Edwin paid me an unaccustomed visit this morning. I haven't called you because I didn't want to wake you up...not your best time of day."

"Why was he here?" Molly asked.

"Edwin said Helene was mentally ill and asked me to call him if she came to classes or rehearsals." Anthony snorted. "Fat chance. He also said he was withdrawing her from the university because she wasn't up to even finishing the term. I was going to call you later to ask if you knew anything about it, but you got here first. I don't trust Edwin an inch, and I'm worried about Helene."

"She's safe. At your house." Molly told him the whole story.

"Let's phone the registrar to see if Edwin's made good his threat," Molly suggested. They did, and found he hadn't.

"Don't you know someone who can check up on this guy, Anthony?" Molly asked. "Surely he has some antecedents. What was he, and where was he, before Helene got mixed up with him? We know he had a previous wife and two children somewhere in the East. I'll bet there are some skeletons in his closet. Maybe having to do with that first family, or there could be other families we know nothing about. If he has this tendency, it would have shown up long before this. How can we find out?"

"I'll phone a friend in Human Resources and see if he can discover whether or not Edwin's credentials and references were checked when he came here," Anthony said.

"For heaven's sake, what's 'Human Resources' and what would it have to do with Edwin's references?"

"It's what used to be called Staffing, and then it was Personnel, Molly," he said as he dialed the phone. "I know you hate it, but it's best to try to keep up with the lingo even if you don't approve of it."

"Everyone seems to have forgotten the KISS method—you know, 'Keep It Simple, Stupid,'" she retorted.

After asking his friend to "make discreet inquiries" and call him back as quickly as possible, Anthony told Molly, as she knew he would, that Helene and Georgia were welcome to stay at his home as long as necessary. He then began making calls to ensure Helene wouldn't be penalized for missing any exams. He got Joey to check her timetable through the computer and was able to notify all her professors she would be absent, for medical reasons, until further notice.

"Now, we've looked after that business. The next thing is to keep those two safe from our madman."

"Anthony, you're a prince. Thank you." Molly hugged him.

"Let's look on the bright side. It's nice to have all this company," he said as he smiled fondly at Molly. "Now go away. Let me get some of this interminable paperwork done, or I won't be able to cook for you tonight. This department is fast falling apart. Trent, now Helene. I can't keep up with all the disasters."

"I haven't told Helene about Trent yet. I figure she's had enough for today. So don't spring it on her as soon as you come home, okay?" Molly warned Anthony. "Have you heard anything from the police or the hospital about Trent?"

"The only thing I could find out is that he's in the ICU. He's at the University Hospital and isn't allowed any visitors."

"Well, keep phoning the hospital. We want to know what's happening," Molly said.

"I will," Anthony assured her. "The boy may be irritating, but he didn't deserve to be knifed."

"By the way, Helene asked me to get her viola and music from her locker, so I'm going down there before I go home. Luckily, this was one of the few times she didn't take it home with her. Now where did I put that combination?" She left the office, fumbling in her pockets for the scrap of paper Helene had given her. On her way past the library, she glanced in and saw Jolene and Ruby with their heads together, poring over a conductor's score. Molly wondered what Sneazewell's wife and Ruby had in common, other than both being violinists. What made them so friendly with one another? Especially since she had seen Sneazewell going into the motel with Ruby. She presumed he was two-timing his wife with her.

After she got Helene's belongings, she passed Agatha, returning to her domain in the library. Did she know the other two women were there? And what they were up to?

Molly drove home to Green Valley looking out for Edwin, fearing he might try to follow her if he knew she was Helene's friend. Not having met him, she didn't know for whom to look, but she didn't see anyone acting suspiciously and didn't think anyone was following her.

When she arrived home, Helene was delighted to see her viola. "At least now I can practice."

"Can I use your computer to send some e-mail?" Georgia asked Molly. "Mom said I couldn't use your phone in case people had caller ID, and I want to let my best friends know I'm safe."

"Sure," Molly replied. "I'm sorry I don't keep any games on the computer for you to use."

"I don't play those silly things, anyway," Georgia replied. "They're no-brainers."

* * *

The next day all the members of the household were rested and in their rooms practicing. Molly had arranged to borrow a cello for Georgia, who suddenly, to Helene's surprise and delight, announced she wished she could practice, too. The phone rang when Helene and Molly were each working on some particularly nasty passages in *Roman Carnival*, Helene in her bedroom, Molly in the living room so as not to bother Ann, who was watching television.

By the time Molly could put down her bass and make it to the phone, the answering machine was taking the call. She turned up the machine to listen to the message.

"You bitch," she heard. "You're interfering where you're not wanted. Go home while you still can."

She picked up the phone. "Who is this and to whom do you think you are speaking?" she demanded, hoping it was a wrong number.

"You. O'Connor woman. Get out of there. You are in my way. Go home. You are not wanted." The voice went on, in what sounded like a computer-generated monotone—or someone disguising the voice.

"I don't have any idea what you're talking about or why you're calling." Molly knew she should just hang up and phone the police, but she was too curious to be prudent.

"You are meddling in someone's life. If you want to keep your own, get out of here."

"Who are you? Only weaklings and cowards make anonymous calls."

"Don't interfere. Stop what you are doing. Leave the city and you won't be harmed. You won't be warned again." The caller hung up.

Molly looked at her phone, hung up, and then grew cold and began shaking. When she could control herself, she phoned the police.

"The call may be connected to a break-in we had two nights ago," she suggested, when she finally found someone who would listen to her complaint, "and I'm wondering if there's any connection with the knifing at Grenoble Episcopal Church. I don't know what police were involved in that. Can you find out?"

They assured her they would pass on her information, "But there isn't anything we can do about crank calls. The only thing we can suggest is for you to buy one of those caller ID phones that show the number of the person phoning you, though that can be blocked, too. Then if he calls again, you may be able to trace him."

After this discouraging response, Molly looked up the police file number they'd been given after the break-in, phoned the person in charge of that business, and passed on the information herself. She'd have to find out who was in charge of the investigation into the knifing of Trent Quillium, too. She felt all these occurrences were in some way connected and wanted to make sure the police had every bit of information she could find to help solve the mystery before someone was murdered.

As she sat wondering what to do, the phone rang. It was Anthony with the good news that Trent Quillium was expected to recover, though he was still in the Intensive Care Unit. He was, however, heavily drugged while a collapsed lung healed and hadn't been able to tell anyone what happened that night.

Molly returned to her practice, but wasn't able to concentrate. Too many questions. Was someone after Anthony? Who wanted her out of the way? And why? To whom did she pose a danger? How did this person know she lived at Anthony's? How much was known about the household? Should she send her mother home, out of range of possible danger? She wished Anthony would hurry home so she could discuss all her questions with him. She didn't want to talk to Helene and Georgia about it. They had enough to worry about, just hiding out from Edwin.

Molly decided to phone Martha, who was looking after her house in Edmonton, to see if everything was okay there. She needed a reassuring dose of home. As she dialed, she reminded herself how lucky she was to have Martha. Her mind replayed the events leading to their fortunate situation.

Martha Winnel worked part-time as a cleaner at Driftwood School when Molly was the librarian there. She was a widow with two children and not much money. Her landlady, Mrs. Tevlin, had been like a fairy godmother to the little family. Molly and Martha became friends when they worked late in the building after school. They discovered they were both from the Peace River country and had heard of one another's families in the way people in small northern communities know about many of even their distant neighbors. Though she'd lost touch with much of what was going on in the community, Molly admired what she knew of Martha's pluck and work ethic.

Though Martha's life had been difficult, and she'd had little time for schooling, Molly discovered she had a thirst for knowledge. As a librarian and generally bookish person, Molly had enjoyed finding books for Martha and her children.

Just after Molly decided to go to Arizona, Martha had phoned. Molly greeted her with great joy and not a little guilt about not having contacted her since she left the school. "I'm delighted to hear from you, Martha. How have you been?"

"Not so good, Miz O'Connor. Miz Tevlin just up and died."

"Oh, no." Molly was shocked. She hadn't been reading the paper or keeping up with obituaries, so wasn't aware of what was going on in the world outside her own grief. She knew Martha depended greatly on Mrs. Tevlin, who had provided a basement apartment for the family in return for Martha doing the gardening in the summer and keeping the walks free of snow and ice in the winter. Her cleaning job at the school paid barely enough to cover her basic expenses, and she was too proud to ask for public assistance. Mrs. Tevlin had cared for Martha's children after school until their mother got home from work, thus saving her child-care fees as well.

"I didn't know she had a bad heart," Martha continued, obviously on the edge of tears. "She never talked about her health. She just went and died, with no warning at all. The children are missing her dreadfully, and so am I. Her nephew from down East came, and he's selling the house. We have to be out of our apartment by the middle of August."

Martha rushed on, speaking quickly as if she was afraid she'd lose confidence. "We're real sad to lose Miz Tevlin, more than the house, but...the fact is, we need a cheap place to rent, and I wondered, do you know anyone who needs a good worker in exchange for a low-rent basement apartment? I don't like to bother you, and anyway, with all your trouble in the last while, you may not be able to help, but...you always said, Miz O'Connor, if I needed help, to call you."

"I'm glad you've called, and I'm sure I can help, Martha," Molly replied before Martha could take a breath and get started again. "Let me think just for a moment." Molly's daughters had offered to look after the house while she was gone, but she wanted someone to live there. The children were busy with their own lives and didn't want to move back home while she was gone. She made up her mind instantly.

"Martha, I'm going away to study for awhile. Would you be interested in moving into my place and looking after it while I'm gone?"

"Goodness sakes." Martha had sounded flustered, hesitated, and then spoke slowly. "I don't know what to say, Miz O'Connor. Are you sure you really need me? You know I'm a hard worker and I don't want charity."

"This isn't charity, Martha. It's mutual need. And this place takes a lot of effort to keep up. My children don't live at home any more and are busy, so I can't just ask them to take over my responsibilities. It would take a great weight off my mind, and theirs, if we knew you were here making sure my home is safe and looked after."

Molly arranged to pick up the Winnels outside the Tevlin house so they could look over her place.

Martha seemed a bit frazzled, but her home-cut brown hair was clean and neat and her worried eyes lit up as Molly alighted from the car. The two women greeted one another. After she'd hugged the children, got them into the car, and made sure they put their seat belts on, Molly marveled at how much Rebecca and Joshua had grown since she saw them last. The children, who were going into grades two and three at school, said they'd never crossed the North Saskatchewan River before. This was a big outing—an adventure. They were silent and wide-eyed during the car ride from their north side lodgings to Molly's home in Belgravia.

Martha wasn't acquainted with the area at all and looked a little unsure about it, as if she were being taken to a brand-new city. Still, she'd managed to move herself from a small farm north of Peace River to the city of Edmonton, so, "I figure I can manage a move across the river in Edmonton," she mumbled to herself as she looked out the car window, enjoying the view of the wide river valley from the High Level Bridge.

Martha seemed pleased when she saw Molly's ranch-style home, built as close to the edges of the lot as the law allowed.

"Not too much front walk to clear of snow in the winter, and not much lawn to mow in the summer," she commented practically.

"You can see I'm not much of a gardener. You'd be welcome to add flowers if you like, but I like the evergreen shrubs and trees because they mostly look after themselves. If you decide to come to live here, you can treat it as your own yard and do what you like."

"I don't know, Miz O'Connor. I haven't had much time for flower gardens. On the farm I had to grow as much of our food as I could. We had a big garden, and it was a lot of work. I think I'd rather just leave this the way it is."

"Whatever you like, Martha, but the option is there. You'll see there's no room for any kind of gardening in the back. The pool takes nearly all of the free space." The children's eyes lit up at the mention of "pool"

The first thing Martha saw inside the house was the old baby grand Chickering piano, Molly's pride and joy, a gift from her father on her fortieth birthday, and a cherished remembrance of him.

"Oh," Martha gasped, "it's so beautiful."

Molly agreed. "Every time I come in the door, I see it and think of my father." The piano's cherry wood and ornate carving never failed to bring her happiness, which is why it had a prominent place in the first room of the house.

Molly in Arizona, waiting for the phone to be answered in Edmonton, suddenly felt a pang in her stomach, a yearning to be back in her own home, enjoying a relatively peaceful life. She visualized herself there now.

Her house didn't have a "front room" or showplace living room, but a "room for living," housing not only the piano, but also a pair of double basses, music stands, and computers with all their attachments, as well as a comfortable couch and matching easy chairs. It contained most of what Molly and Paul had considered essential in their lives.

Next to this first enormous room was the kitchen, with its full-length French doors opening out to the screened deck and ultimately to the long, narrow swimming pool that took up most of the land in the back. The kitchen had an island working area and was equipped with a microwave and double self-cleaning ovens. Beyond the kitchen was a full-sized dining room big enough to comfortably handle a dozen guests, or twenty at a pinch. Molly and Paul had enjoyed entertaining and used the room frequently.

As Martha looked around the house, she voiced apprehension. Perhaps it was too grand for her to look after properly. Molly pretended she didn't hear Martha's mumblings and continued the tour.

In the basement, there was a suite with large windows making it bright and welcoming. For fire safety reasons, a door from the main basement bedroom opened on to steps leading from the basement directly to the back yard.

For several years, the suite had been used by Molly's children when they reached university age. Now that they all had their own apartments, the rooms were empty and looked as if they needed occupants to bring them back to life.

Martha observed her children peering out the windows at the swimming pool, twitching in anticipation of water games and this bright new space to live in. When she saw the excitement in their eyes, she squared her shoulders and announced, "You just show me what to do with that pool, and I'll do my best to look after your place, Miz O'Connor."

Molly breathed a sigh of relief.

Martha and her family moved in the next week.

* * *

Molly dragged her mind back to the present and Arizona in time to greet Martha cheerily when she answered the phone on the fourth ring.

"I'm sorry I haven't called in so long, Martha," Molly began. "I've been totally immersed in my classes and orchestra, having a very selfish time."

"That's okay. Everything's been fine here, Miz O'Connor," Martha assured her, "except for a funny call I didn't rightly understand. I didn't know whether to call you about it, but I don't like to call long distance unless it's an emergency. Funny you should call. Today I just got to thinking I should talk to someone about it. In fact, I thought I should phone that nice detective from when your man was killed. You know, that Mr. Donegan."

"Tell me about the call," Molly broke in, wondering if it had anything to do with the call she'd received in Green Valley.

"It was last night it came. I wasn't sure if it was a man with a high voice or a woman with a low voice, and whoever it was, say it was a man, well, he wanted to know how to get in touch with you. I told him you were in Arizona, and he said he'd like to phone you, what's your number there, and I told him. Then he asked me how long you were planning to be there, and then I started getting suspicious, and I wondered was he a friend of yours and, if he was, how come he didn't already know. So then I started asking him questions, like, hadn't you told him, and could I tell you he'd called, and he was suddenly in a big hurry to get off the phone. I hope I didn't offend a real friend of yours. Did he call you?" Martha sounded worried.

"No, Martha, no friend called. But there's no harm done," she said, hoping there wasn't. At least, that solved part of the puzzle of the nasty call she'd had.

"But just when I was going to call Mr. Donegan about it, you know, the detective, well, he called here. He wanted to know how you were, and I told him you were okay, last I heard. I told him about the phone call, and he said just don't give out information any more, just take numbers and call you. He left his home number, and another number, and said to give them to you next time I heard from you, and you was to call him if you needed him for anything."

"Thank you, Martha. That's good news." Molly was so relieved to hear the message, she almost forgot to write down the numbers Martha gave her.

"Just one more thing I gotta talk about," Martha went on. "I hate to ask, but the kids want it so bad. Joshua found a scruffy looking little kitten on the front doorstep this morning, and it was still there when he came home from school at noon. It's an ugly looking little thing with a big bushy tail. Looks like a squirrel. Joshua wants to know if he can keep it, look after it, eh? I told him I didn't think so, but I'd ask you."

"Of course he can, Martha. I love cats, but Paul was allergic to them so we couldn't have one. By all means let Joshua adopt it, but make sure you get all the shots, and get it fixed as soon as it's old enough. Use some of that 'cushion money' I left in your account. We don't want to start a colony of cats if we can help it."

"I'll do it right away. He'll be real happy with the news."

They made arrangements about the animal and finished off with Molly reminding Martha to phone her anytime if something came up and not to worry about the expense. "Don't give my phone number out to anyone except Brian Donegan, okay?"

"I'm real sorry about giving it away to that other one."

Molly assured her she wasn't upset, and they rang off. She looked at the phone numbers she'd written down for Brian and decided to call him right away, even though he probably wouldn't be home. He had been so levelheaded and kind when he was in charge of investigating Paul's murder. And he knew her well enough to know she didn't make up stories—wasn't a "fuzzy-headed dame," as the local police obviously thought she was. He'd know what to do. She desperately needed to talk to him and wished he were in Green Valley right now.

She rang his home number first, expecting to get an answering machine, and was delighted when he picked up the instrument on the first ring.

"How did I manage to be lucky enough to find you at home?" Molly asked. "I thought detectives were never at home."

Brian laughed. "I was up most of the night working on a case, so I'm home catching up on my sleep. I'm glad to hear from you. I gave my number to Martha to pass on just last night. She's very efficient." His voice took on a concerned tone. "Is the caller who was asking her about you harassing you? Are you having any problems down there?"

Molly felt such relief at hearing his voice, she nearly cried. She spent the next half hour giving Brian a detailed account of all the peculiar things that had been happening in Tucson and Green Valley—Anthony's accident, Trent Quillium knifed and collapsed at the concert, the break-in at Anthony's, and the threatening phone call.

"You're a good listener, Brian. I feel better just for having told you all about it," she said, when she finally finished.

"As a matter of fact, I have a little time off coming to me. I think I'll take it and come down for a couple of weeks. I'll call a friend I have on the police force in Tucson. Are there motels near you in Green Valley?"

"I don't know. Can you believe I've never noticed, or even thought about it? I'll find out and phone you. I'm sure everyone around here would love to meet you. Does your friend here have contacts with the local police who look after Green Valley? Someone who'll know what we should do or to whom we should talk here. In fact, when you're talking with your friend, can you see if you can find out if an Edwin Hanson has a criminal record, or where he came from, and anything about his previous wife?" Molly told him about Helene and Georgia. "Anything you can learn will help. I know you police detectives have your own devious ways of getting information," Molly teased him, but then quickly made sure he knew her request was serious, "and, frankly, we're desperate here. I'm so afraid that jerk is going to hurt Helene and Georgia, or maybe even us if he finds out they're here. I'm sure he must have done something before. This couldn't be a sudden aberration."

"I'll find out all I can and let you know as soon as I have anything. Meanwhile, I'll make some plane reservations. I'll join you as soon as I can get away. Try not to let anyone get murdered before I come, okay?" he joked.

"At the rate I've been going in the last year, that isn't funny," Molly replied. She was not amused. She gave him Anthony's phone number and said good-bye.

Chapter 10

"Ohh," Ann exclaimed and stepped back from the open window. She'd just raised the blinds in her bedroom and been confronted by a swarthy face on the other side of the metal bars that covered every window of Anthony's house. The muscular young man looked just as startled as she was. "What are you doing here?" Ann demanded, the bars on the windows giving her courage.

"Por favor, Señora," he ventured, looking frightened himself, "the señor, he is here?"

"What do you want with the señor?" Ann didn't want to let him know she, Helene, and Georgia were in the house alone, both Molly and Anthony being at the university.

"The señor with the broken head." The man rubbed the back of his head.

Ann understood he was referring to Anthony's pool accident.

"You mean Mr. Clint. He's fine. Do you know him?"

"He is a kind man. He leaves water for my people…at the wall…by the house. In the summer we need water. In the desert, man soon be dead without water. He is a good man. He know suffering."

"What does that have to do with his broken head? Were you here the night he was injured by the pool?" Ann asked, wondering if he had not only been around but had also been responsible for the injury.

"No, no, no, Señora, we no hurt the man from this house. But I go from the fields where I work, earn money for my family. I pass here in the night. I see the car behind the house, not the señor's car. I hear voices near the water. I hear something hit the water. I see the señora run to the car, get in the car, go fast away. I look over the fence. Señor is with his face in the water, not move. I come in the yard, go in the water, pull him out. There is blood. I am afraid. If someone see me, they think I hurt him. We get always the blame. So I ring the bell. I hope someone help, but I run away. Then I feel bad. This señor, he good to us. I not so good to him."

"If your story is true, you may have saved his life," Ann said. "He would have drowned if he'd been left in the pool. Maybe the person hit him and left him to die. Did you get a look at who it was? Are you sure it was a woman?"

"I think a woman, but there are clouds on the moon. Who know? Much hair. Jeans. All have jeans."

"And men and women have long hair. I see your problem," Ann responded. "Thank you for telling me. I will speak to Mr. Clint about it. Will you be back?"

"No, no, no, I go home now. It is good the señor is okay. Gracias, Señora."

Ann heard Helene calling her to lunch. The man must have heard the voice, too, for he disappeared from her window without a backward glance. Ann hoped he had a safe journey home.

"Did I hear you talking to someone?" Helene asked as she came into Ann's room to make sure she'd heard the call to lunch.

"Yes," Ann replied, "a very important little chat." She began to relate the story as they went to the kitchen, and had to repeat it when Georgia came in. Georgia was using Molly's computer to write a detailed account of her experience with her stepfather, a therapy suggested by Ann, who knew that sexual abuse affected a young girl for the rest of her life. She hoped that writing and talking about it might reduce its long-term effects by providing an outlet for Georgia to vent her rage.

Ann was enjoying their company. Even the sound of Helene practicing five or more hours every day warmed her heart. Molly and Anthony were gone much of the time, and she loved having people around. She'd even entertained the thought she might start taking walks, hoping to meet other walkers, but she didn't expect to get quite that desperate. Perhaps a drive down to the nearby seniors' recreation center would be a better ploy, if they'd let her join as a visitor. But now she had company and didn't feel the need of anything else.

Georgia had quickly succumbed to Ann's sympathetic ear and nurturing spirit. She began pouring out the story of life with her stepfather.

She and her mother had already experienced rocky times after Georgia's father left many years before. They'd had no financial help while Helene worked and went to university. With student loans hanging over her head, Helene got a job teaching in Edmonton, where she had been taking her degree. She worked at temporary summer jobs to help boost their income during school vacations. When Helene married Edwin, she'd seemed so happy Georgia didn't want to say anything to spoil it. But she had seen how the man looked at her right from the start and didn't trust him.

Helene and Georgia were still very much afraid of what Edwin might do. They'd read so much in newspapers and seen programs on television about thwarted people who murdered their own families. They thought Edwin's warped mind might make him capable of injuring them yet.

* * *

When Molly returned from her class at the university, Ann told her the story she'd heard from the young Mexican man at her window. They decided to wait until after supper and Anthony's daily AA meeting before they talked to him about it.

"What do you make of it?" Molly asked Anthony later, after Ann had told him about the visitor. "Could it be true? Could someone have tried to kill you?"

"I can't think why," Anthony replied, "and unfortunately, I can't remember anything from that night. But I used to have a swim before I went to bed, many times when I was drunk, and I haven't lost my step before. I've always wondered what happened that night. Did you ask him to describe the car?" Anthony directed the question to Ann.

"Oh, Anthony, I am sorry. I just don't think about cars. I should have asked, shouldn't I? I wouldn't make a very good detective," Ann said, looking contrite. She was very good at getting to know everything about people; however, mechanical things interested her only insofar as they helped to make her life comfortable. Molly suspected her mother had carefully preserved her ignorance of those things she didn't want to deal with so family and friends could look after them for her.

"The young man was quite sweet in his concern for you, Anthony, and told me he and others appreciated your kindness to them."

"I'm not really that kind, though I wish I could take credit for being so," said Anthony. "I just feel if this is the way the poor buggers have to live, I'm not going to make it harder for them, but I don't want them coming into the yard or house, looking for food or water, or maybe taking something they think we don't need, since we have so much and they so little. So it's as much self-preservation as altruism, I'm afraid."

"Whatever it is, it may have saved your life, you old fool. I'm so glad you're off the sauce now," Molly said, "and, if I were you, I'd look behind me in dark places. Someone doesn't like you."

"Of course there are people who don't like me. You can't be head of any department of any faculty of any university without making enemies. No matter how fair you think you're being, or how diligent you are about your job, there are always people who don't agree with what you're doing, or don't think you've done the right thing by them. And, of course, there are those who are ambitious and want your job, whether they're capable of doing it or not. I've never been deluded enough to think I'm well-loved," Anthony said indignantly.

"But you never know for sure how well balanced those ambitious types are. And, Anthony, every hierarchy gets stuck with the power-hungry. Whether they're competent or not, they use whatever means necessary to get to the next step." Molly shook her head and continued. "Desire for power—power through position—is dangerous. I've watched too many people get to the top by rather devious means. I've lost respect for position. The higher they get, the worse they get. Some famous person, I can never remember who, said, 'Power corrupts and absolute power corrupts absolutely.'"

"First Baron Acton, dear, from a letter he wrote in the 1800s, and it was 'Power tends to corrupt and absolute power corrupts absolutely.' I seem to recall Churchill quoting that during the war," Ann commented. "I can't remember why he said it, but there were certainly a lot of corrupt people around Hitler and his lot at the time, and they certainly had too much power."

"Powerful people might once have been relatively decent people, but too soon they forget the human element, become too impressed with their own persona. They could be driven to kill someone who was in their way, if they got impatient enough," Molly said.

"But there are some very good people at the top, Molly," Ann said, not wanting her heroes stomped upon. She was of the generation that revered doctors, lawyers, heads of state, companies, and people of great wealth. "I don't like you being quite so critical of everyone. I think they must have great ability."

"I won't deny that, Mother. Many in top positions got there through their worth and ability," Molly said impatiently. "We're not damning them all, though I suppose it sounds like we are. But working with the other kind, the power-hungry, is very unsettling. I don't trust them an inch."

"Aren't we getting a little far from the problem?" Helene asked, after having sat quietly for most of the evening. "You're back on your soapbox, Molly. Anthony's welfare is where we started."

"Right, Helene," said Molly, and turned back to Anthony. "So, who in your department would like your job enough to bump you off?"

"There are some who think an 'old pouf' shouldn't have the job," Anthony said.

"Oh, Anthony, surely not in this day and age," Molly responded.

"Sometimes I think you are the most naive person I know, Molly." Anthony laughed. "Yes, there are still people with prejudices against gays, blacks, women, Mexicans, any foreigners, short people, tall people, and yes, Ann, even old people—anyone they feel they can bully in order to bolster their own self-confidence."

"I guess I really do know that. I just don't like to think about it," Molly admitted. "Do you suppose these other strange occurrences are in any way related to your pool injury? Like Trent Quillium, poor kid. Why was he attacked? Does it have anything to do with you? Even old Sneazewell would have to agree it is definitely overreacting to stab a musician just because he's irritating."

"Actually, Trent had an appointment to see me the morning after the recital. I assumed it was about his graduation recital or something to do with his courses. Now, with Ann's information, I suppose I should mention it to the police, in case it has some bearing on the attack. I'll do that in the morning. I did check with the hospital, and the poor lad is still in intensive care."

"What about our Sneazewell? I'd love to cast him as the villain. What a creep he is. Why did you ever hire him?" Molly asked.

"I had no choice. The man is brilliant, highly qualified, and his wife is the daughter of the Dean of Arts, Dean Kaiser. If he hadn't the credentials, I could somehow have overcome the connection to the dean, but my hands were tied."

"The man's an ass," Molly announced. "Surely even the dean can see that."

"Don't be crude, Molly," Ann admonished as she picked up her knitting. "It only indicates a limited vocabulary. I'm sure you can find other words to describe the poor little man."

"He is definitely not a poor little man, Mother. He is a degenerate, bullying, sadistic, insulting, horrid little man." Molly got up and stretched. "He doesn't belong in any position of power."

"Unfortunately, I could hardly tell Dean Kaiser his son-in-law is all that and more. Perhaps the dean wanted his daughter nearby to watch over her. If I had a daughter married to Sneazewell, I would," Anthony said, and rubbed his bearded face. "Sneazewell would like to have my job, too. He wants complete and utter power in the department. But I don't think even the dean can give him that without faculty approval, and he'd never get it."

"Does Sneazewell seriously think getting your job is a possibility?" Molly asked, her voice reflecting her revulsion at the thought of Sneazewell in charge.

"Yes, and I suspect most people with an ego the size of his believe they can do anything they want, and just walk over everyone until they get it," Anthony replied, shrugging his shoulders.

"When's your appointment up, Anthony?"

"At the end of next year, and I'll be very glad to be out of it. I want a different life. I'm even thinking about retiring early."

"That means if someone is after your job, he or she is in a very big hurry."

"I'm tired of thinking about it. Let's go for a swim and try for an early bedtime," Anthony suggested.

"I'm glad you're being smart about making sure someone else is with you when you swim since your accident," Molly responded.

Helene had become very quiet again. Molly thought she was probably wondering about her own future, feeling in a sort of limbo here at Anthony's.

"Come join us," Molly encouraged her. "It'll take your mind off your worries."

They invited Georgia to swim with them, too, and Ann condescended to try the hot tub next to the pool. In consideration of their guests, Anthony wore his bathing suit.

Chapter 11

The dress rehearsal for the orchestra's end-of-term performance took place in the Crebel Auditorium, a separate structure attached to the music building by a covered walkway. Glen Quaverville, in his freshman year, was already concertmaster, or principal first violin, of the orchestra. He also carried the traditional title of assistant conductor, but he'd had no opportunity to exercise himself in this capacity under the direction of Dr. Sneazewell. He was sure Sneazewell was afraid to be absent from rehearsal for any reason because he, Glen, could do a better job. Sneazewell would never allow anyone to show him up.

Glen knew he was a very talented and accomplished violinist. He'd won many prizes and scholarships. He was sure he belonged at one of the big eastern schools, such as Juilliard or Curtis, and was just biding his time in this place until he made the right connections and got the right backing. He could not afford to go to New York to audition without it.

Glen's method of approaching people and businesses for financial assistance, however, had been so aggressive and egotistical they always turned him down, in spite of his obvious ability and need. Resentful about his lack of success, he never suspected he had only himself to blame. Glen's parents had always made sure he had good teachers, or the best they could get for him in what he considered their cultural outback. Glen barely acknowledged the fact they'd remortgaged their little house to buy him a decent violin, just as he tended to take for granted they should deny themselves holidays and other frills to see he got the best they could provide. They didn't have anything left to give. He wanted more.

Tall, blond, and muscular, Glen had difficulty keeping his lip from curling in disdain as he watched Sneazewell make his way to the podium. The man was the epitome of decadence. Glen couldn't understand how he got this plummy university job. Sneazewell might be brilliant, and he might at one time have been presentable, but in Glen's opinion, he was unworthy. One of these days the man would surely pop a blood vessel during one of his rages and die right there on the podium.

The rehearsal began on time. As his fingers flew across the violin strings, Glen's highly developed hand, eye, and finger coordination was wonderful to behold. He felt the flush of adrenalin that always came when he knew he was in complete control. I'll show everyone someday, he thought, as he perfectly executed a particularly difficult passage of music the rest of the section blew. I will be a great conductor as well as a magnificent violinist. And people like Sneazewell won't have a chance.

Sneazewell stopped the orchestra to harangue the violin section. "I need one of those stomach tablets I see you chewing all the time, Quaverville." He grabbed the package from Glen's music stand, removed a couple of tablets, and chewed them rapidly. "I'll keep the package. The way these gorillas parading as musicians play, I may need more." The rehearsal continued.

It was amazing Sneazewell didn't feel the ooze of ill feeling building up against him. As the rehearsal continued, Glen observed his disgusting habit of licking his filthy thumb before he turned each page of the score. It made his stomach turn. And Sneazewell had his pills. The cheapskate. He'd soon learn it was better to buy his own.

* * *

The older she got, the longer it seemed to take Molly to pack up her bass at the end of rehearsals, and the more tired she felt after two hours of concentration. They'd just finished playing *Till Eulenspiegel* by Richard Strauss. Most Strauss was extremely difficult for her to play, and she was very tense. She remembered reading somewhere that Strauss had not liked the way modern orchestras played his music, as he had intended many of the difficult passages to be an effect, not the accurate rendition of every note most modern conductors insisted upon. Molly was sure her performance would be more to Strauss's liking. The piece was being taken at too great a speed for her to get all the notes, no matter how much she practiced.

Andrew Penwith was in his freshman year. As he packed his bass with jerky movements, he kept flinging his dyed black hair off his face, his whole body radiating anger. He looked at Molly placidly pulling the cover over her bass and said, "I'm waiting to talk to Sneazewell. That bastard should have placed me in the first chair of this section, not the fourth. You must have noticed that. It should be obvious to everyone." He looked at the conductor still at the podium talking to Glen Quaverville. "I'm going to demand a re-audition for positions in the bass section, and Sneazewell better not turn me down."

He carefully packed his bow in a hard case and put it in the special pocket of the bass cover. "I don't know how you can stand this place," he chided her. "You don't need to jump through these hoops. Why do you bother?"

"I hate to tell you this, Andrew, but I actually enjoy it. Well, most of it, anyway." Molly smiled sympathetically, not envying the boy either his youth or his anger.

"I see you trotting off diligently to all those boring classes, looking very smug. I thought you were just doing your duty." Andrew put his bow in its case as he talked. "Classes are such a waste of time. I don't need to go and listen to endless lectures. I just read the stuff up in the text the night before the exams. But these effing rehearsals. If you miss any, old Sneazewell gives you a low mark and you're dead meat. I thought we'd be finished with attendance taking in high school, for God's sake." He finished his tirade, put his bass down carefully, and strode purposefully over to the podium.

Molly felt sad for the youthful students who were full of contempt for their university life. She wished they could enjoy it even half as much as she did now. She wondered if students should be required to work for a year or so before being allowed into a university. Maybe it would seem a little more special to them. She remembered wasting a lot of time in her own first year. The older she got, the more she remembered the difficulties of those years, and the happier she was to be past them.

She paused in her packing to watch Andrew Penwith talking to Sneazewell, who was fussily turning the pages of his score. Lick, turn, lick, turn—such an ugly habit, she thought. He was ignoring Penwith as he visibly became more and more angry. She saw Penwith turn abruptly away and return to his bass. He picked it up and left the hall. She was relieved to see he was careful with the instrument even in his agitated state.

When Molly next looked up from her packing, she saw Sneazewell clutching at his neck, a frantic expression on his face. Glen Quaverville, sitting in his chair nearby, seemed oblivious to Sneazewell's distress. Molly put her bass down quickly and started over to see if she could help, but before she got very far, Sneazewell suddenly staggered and fell backwards off the podium and stage. There was a thud and a sickening cracking sound.

Agatha and Jolene, who had been picking up music from the stands, reached the edge of the stage at the same time as Molly and Glen. They all stood transfixed by what they saw. It looked as if Sneazewell's head had hit the edge of one of the front-row seats.

Ruby, sitting in an audience chair not far from where Sneazewell fell, appeared unaware of the confusion and finished zipping up her violin case before turning around. Then, seeing the conductor flat on his back on the floor with his head at an awkward angle, she began screaming hysterically.

Molly suddenly felt like the character in old L'il Abner comics, from the fifties, who carried a black cloud above his head and brought disaster with him wherever he went. She wasn't responsible for any of the disasters, but she was beginning to feel, albeit unreasonably, as if her presence brought them on.

"I'll go phone for an ambulance," she said, and ran off to the bank of phones in the lobby.

When she came back into the hall, the musicians standing around Sneazewell told her he was dead. Jolene and Agatha had already returned to the stage, where they were collecting the scores from Dr. Sneazewell's stand and adding them to the pile of music they'd already taken from the musicians' stands. Were they in shock, behaving as if nothing had happened? Molly ran up the stairs to the stage and approached them.

"I'm not sure you should be moving or touching anything until the police come," Molly said.

"What an odd remark," Agatha responded, looking surprised. "The music has nothing to do with this. It isn't as if Sneazewell was murdered. He just fell off the stage."

"But why did he fall off the stage?" Molly asked, disconcerted by Agatha's apparent callousness.

"It was obviously an accident," Agatha replied. "Who knows why accidents happen? Do any of us care what happened to him?"

"Actually," Molly said, becoming angry, "I do. Yes, he was an obnoxious little man, but he was a living human being and now he's dead. Yes. I care."

Agatha shrugged her shoulders and turned to Jolene. Molly overheard Jolene saying, "She probably just reads too many murder mysteries. Ignore her. Here, I might as well help you carry the music back to the library. There's nothing I can do waiting around here." Jolene took half of Agatha's load, and they left the hall.

Molly was surprised and disturbed by Jolene's odd behavior. Even though Sneazewell had never, in the orchestra, acknowledged Jolene as his wife, and was openly contemptuous of her as a musician, she was surprised the woman could be so incredibly blasé about his death, even if she was glad to be rid of him. But if she had wanted to be free of him, she could easily have just divorced him, Molly thought, so since she hadn't, she must have found his behavior acceptable.

When the ambulance arrived, it was obvious nothing could be done for Sneazewell. The attendants asked everyone to remain in the hall until the police arrived.

Molly told them she was taking her instrument to her locker and would be back. It was a good excuse, she thought, to find out what Jolene and Agatha were up to, since the locker was near the library. She wanted to see what was keeping them so long. They should have returned by now.

As she wheeled her bass out of the auditorium and down the long corridor leading to the rehearsal room, lockers, and library, it felt spooky. Molly didn't like being in this part of the building alone and missed having Helene for company, to keep her fear of the dark shadows at bay. She'd missed walking through the halls, talking about their classes and rehearsals with her old friend. It was too quiet with so few people around.

She thought about Brian Donegan and hoped he would be arriving soon. He had been so comforting when Paul was killed. He would know what she should do about her suspicions. She wondered if he had any information about Edwin yet, and wished poor Helene could return to the university. She'd already missed one exam and would hate to miss them all and the concert as well.

Molly's trip to the locker and back was uneventful, and she chided herself for being so nervous. She hadn't seen Jolene and Agatha, and the library was closed when she went down the hall to check after putting away her bass. They were in the auditorium when she returned, and she wondered what route they had taken. They would have passed her if they had gone directly to and from the library.

"Who saw what happened here?" the officer in charge was asking when she returned. Both the campus and city police were standing around the dead man, talking in quiet voices.

Glen Quaverville was the first to volunteer information.

"One of the bass players had been talking to him, and had just stomped off," he began. "Andrew. Andrew Penwith, it was. I didn't pay attention to what they were saying, but Andrew was really angry. Jolene and Agatha were standing near the podium picking up music from the stands. I was busy with my music, but from the corner of my eye I saw him grab his throat, as if he was choking or couldn't get his breath somehow. When I looked up, I saw his eyes were kind of bulging. Then he just seemed to stagger back off the podium. He blacked out or something, lost his balance, and crashed to the floor. It happened so quickly, he was down before I could do anything to stop him." Now back in his chair on the stage, Glen was sitting with his elbows resting on his knees. Suddenly, he leaned over and covered his face with his hands, as if he couldn't bear to look in the direction where Dr. Sneazewell's body still lay. Though he'd often wished him dead, he didn't like to see the actual fact.

Agatha and Jolene were sitting side-by-side in the viola section chairs.

"I didn't see anything at all," Agatha volunteered, "but I wasn't looking at him. I was picking up music off the stands and had my back to him. The first realization I had that anything was wrong was when I heard the noise of his fall."

"Didn't you hear him gasping for breath?" Glen looked at her. "You weren't that far from him."

"No, I was talking to Jolene, asking her to go get the bass music."

"And I was on the way over to do what she asked," Jolene added.

"What does it matter? The man fell. It looked to me like he broke his neck when he fell," Agatha said.

Glen was ashen. He looked as if he might throw up at any moment.

"But why did he fall?" Molly said. "I expect the autopsy will tell them."

"You have to do an autopsy even though it's obvious how he died?" Agatha asked the police.

"Yes, ma'am," an officer replied. He looked about junior-high-school age to Molly.

Ruby Reddick was sitting, sobbing, in the chair behind Glen.

"Is that woman a relative of the deceased?" one of the older police-men asked Glen. This one looked to Molly as if he might have lived long enough to be in high school.

"No. But I think they were friends," he replied.

"Good friends," Agatha piped up, with a sneer on her face.

The police all looked suspiciously at her, then turned their attention to Molly. She explained who she was. The youngest took all their names and told them they could go. Molly lingered to speak with him after the others left.

"I just wanted to mention to you there have been several unexplained things happening to members of the music department, and this might be related to them."

"More accidents?" the young officer asked, raising his eyebrows at her.

"Accidental and deliberate injuries and some we're not certain about. Nevertheless, they all happened to members of the music department, so it's pretty suspicious. First of all, the chairman of the music department nearly drowned in his own pool in early October. That could have been an accident or a deliberate attempt on his life."

"Was that reported to the police?"

"No. At the time we thought it was an accident. However, we've recently had a witness tell us he saw someone leaving the place in a car just after it happened, and that, coupled with the attempted murder of one of our cellists, Trent Quillium, last week, leads us to believe it was no accident. Trent was knifed near a church in Tucson where we were attending a concert put on by members of the music department. He managed to stumble into the performance before collapsing in front of us all. That same night, our house in Green Valley was trashed." Molly didn't mention Helene's problems, believing they couldn't have anything to do with this business. "And now Dr. Sneazewell. No one liked him, and he made many enemies in this orchestra. That was his wife with her good friend, the librarian. And the girl who was crying, Ruby Reddick, was not his wife, but was having an affair with Sneazewell, I think."

The officer looked at her as if he thought she was trying to be the local Miss Marple. He listened politely and made notes just in case some of her information was relevant, but obviously didn't see this death as being anything but accidental.

"How do you know so much about all of them?" he asked politely, but Molly heard the smirk in his tone of voice, the implication she was just an old busybody.

"Because to most of these young students, I'm an old lady...like a wall...of no account." He should understand how they feel, she thought, since this appeared to be his own opinion of her. "So I hear and see things. And I just happened to be around when all these things occurred. Anyway," she got up from the chair she'd been resting in, "you have my name and phone number if any of this is information you can use, and you want to ask me about it." She took her leave, feeling frustrated, knowing what she'd told him would probably remain in his notebook and never get passed on to the right person. She decided to phone Brian again as soon as she got home.

As Molly walked to her car in the parkade, she had the eerie feeling she was being watched. She wished she had asked one of the campus police to accompany her, but they all seemed busy, and she was embarrassed to ask the officers for anything when the one with whom she'd spoken clearly thought her a silly old woman. By the time she got to her car, she was practically running. Her heart seemed to be beating in her throat as she climbed in quickly and locked the doors. Every shadow in the parking lot represented a threat to her, and she prayed for the car to start with no difficulty. Her fear made her imagine even this always reliable vehicle might let her down.

Of course it started, and she felt foolish. But then, as she backed out of her parking stall, she thought she saw someone running toward her. She floored the accelerator. The car bucked and then zoomed off to the exit, bouncing over the speed bumps. There, she was held up by having to insert her card to open the gate. Once she was out, she felt a little safer. Who was running toward the car? Was someone after her? Might it be Edwin?

Molly took only main streets through the city. She didn't want to be caught in any dark places where she could be easily followed or ambushed. She felt a little safer as she drove up the ramp and on to the freeway. There she concentrated on trying to determine if any car followed her. She sped up, then slowed down. She even took the off ramp from the freeway at one point, drove through the underpass and back up the on ramp on the other side to continue on the freeway. If she was being followed, it was being done very well. She couldn't detect any one vehicle consistently behind her.

By the time she reached Green Valley, Molly's heartbeat was almost normal. With a sob of relief, she drove into Anthony's driveway, parked the car, and unlocked the door to the house without seeing anyone in the shadows, or any cars driving up behind her. When she was safely inside with the door locked behind her, she collapsed into a kitchen chair.

"What's happened?" Helene was in the kitchen making popcorn.

She'd been startled when Molly rushed in the door, but relieved when she saw who it was. "You look like you've just seen a ghost."

"Overactive imagination," Molly explained, taking deep breaths. "I know I wasn't followed home, and I know there's no threat, now that I'm safely here. But I feel as if I've been running for my life. My imagination is playing nasty games with me."

"Hey, don't be down on yourself," Helene commiserated. "Ever since we got away from Edwin, every noise I hear, I think it's him coming to get at Georgia or me. We need a good dose of normal." She went back to her popcorn making.

Anthony came into the kitchen. "You look a mess," he commented. "Has it been a bad day?"

"Thanks for the compliment, you rat. That's no way to make a woman feel good," Molly chastised him. "And yes, it's been a helluva day. Dr. Sneazewell is dead. It happened right after the orchestra rehearsal, and I don't believe it's the accident the police, and everyone else, seem to think it was. There have been too many so-called accidents lately."

"Good God," Anthony said, "why didn't you phone me to come and get you, you silly woman? With all that's been going on, I don't think any of us should be around that place, or anywhere else, alone."

"Granted, I was terrified coming home," Molly replied as she took off her sweater and shoes and started hunting for something to eat. She wished she could have a large glass of good wine but although Anthony had assured her she could, she didn't want to be responsible for him failing in his attempt to keep away from booze. Damn Anthony's problem with alcohol, she thought uncharitably.

"How did he die?" Anthony asked as he propelled her away from the refrigerator and sat her down at the kitchen table. "Tell us what happened." He found Molly's portion of supper and put it in the microwave to heat. He'd made a roast and mashed potatoes, and when she smelled the food warming, Molly was suddenly starving.

"I was packing up my instrument, off in the bass section. He was on the podium looking angry, which he usually is...was. But the next time I looked at him, he was behaving as if he couldn't breathe or was having some sort of attack, and then he fell off the stage. Too bad the new podium you wanted made, with the bar around the back of the conductor, wasn't built on time. It would have kept him from falling off the stage," she said. "But I strongly suspect he was in very serious trouble before he fell. Maybe a stroke or a heart attack. God knows, he's always having fits," Molly continued, tucking into the food as soon as it came out of the microwave. "And I just remembered. He grabbed a package of tablets off Glen Quaverville's stand after telling us our playing was so bad he needed Glen's stomach pills—this was not long before the end of the rehearsal. He crammed a couple of them into his mouth right away and chewed for awhile before making another nasty comment to the orchestra and continuing the rehearsal," she said through a mouthful of supper.

"Finish your food first, dear," Ann piped up as she came into the kitchen. "Don't speak with your mouth full."

Molly sent her a look needing no words. Ann got the point, and sat down.

"The police are still there?" Anthony asked, as he took a side bowl of salad from the refrigerator and gave it to Molly.

"They were when I left." Molly started on the salad.

"I think I'd better get over there." Anthony collected his car keys and started for the door.

"I thought no one was going anywhere alone anymore," Molly said to his back. "You just made the suggestion."

"That was for you women," Anthony replied as he opened the door.

"Sexist," Molly said, disgusted, getting up and following him to the door, fork in hand. "It wasn't me who got her head bashed in at the swimming pool. Stay here, you fool. I'm not going to get a decent night's rest if I know you're over at the university in that spooky auditorium when everyone else with any sense has gone home."

Anthony paused and looked at Molly with surprise. "You really are worried about me, aren't you?"

"Of course, you idiot. Would you kindly stay here? I've had enough for tonight."

"All right. But I'd better phone Dean Kaiser in case he hasn't been called already," Anthony relented.

"As soon as you get off the phone, I'm calling Brian again," Molly told him. "He said he might come down, and he was going to look into Edwin's past. I wish he were here now. He said he has a friend who's a detective with the Tucson police force. I'll feel a lot more confident when he comes to talk to them. They'll listen to him, where they just ignore me. They think I'm a silly old bag," she said, still miffed at being discounted. "By the way, Anthony, is there a motel near here? Brian wants one near us. Other than the gorgeous sunsets and desert flora and fauna, all I notice when I'm driving home is those copper mine tailings on the west side of the road."

"That's from the arsenic they use to extract the copper. The leavings won't support much growth so they can't cover it up," Anthony, ever the teacher, explained in a distracted voice as he looked up Dean Kaiser's phone number. "Did it look like Dr. Sneazewell had been poisoned?"

"It could have been anything. I expect they'll do an autopsy. But what about a motel?"

"Brian doesn't need a motel. He can stay here. The sofa makes out into a bed." Anthony, hospitable as ever, was sure he could fit an army into his big house, so empty until Molly came.

"I can move into the queen-size bed with Mom in her room, and he can have my bedroom. Mom and I have shared a bed before. She won't mind, and he'll be more comfortable with a room of his own. We'll all feel a lot safer with the two of you here. I'll tell him when I phone."

"Go ahead and use the phone first." Anthony gave her the instrument. "I can see you're chomping at the bit. I'll call the dean after."

Molly dialed Brian's home number. "I'm so glad I got you at home again," she said when he answered, "two times in a row."

"That's because I'm packing to fly down tomorrow. I leave on the early morning Delta flight and arrive in Tucson about four in the afternoon."

"Thank heavens. Anthony has invited you to stay here with the rest of the menagerie he's acquired. You even get your own room. We need your brains and your presence. We're all scared out of our trees. Another supposed accident tonight, and this time the guy is dead, and I'm worried about who will be next."

"Who's dead?" Brian asked apprehensively.

"The obnoxious conductor of our orchestra. Another music department casualty."

"I'm glad it was none of you. Are you sure I should stay there? It sounds like a full house," Brian asked. Molly assured him the house was big enough, and they'd all be happier with another man guarding the place. He told her not to bother coming to the plane. He planned to rent a car when he arrived. Molly gave him detailed instructions on how to get to Anthony's place in Green Valley.

"I might be a little late getting there. I'm going to stop at the police station first to meet with Don Jennings—he's the detective friend I told you about. He's going to fill me in on what they have to date, so don't plan any supper for me, either. We'll probably eat together in the city."

"Just bring your Don Jennings along. We have three cooks here. Not me, as you already know. But my mother, Anthony, and Helene are all super chefs, adept at preparing a sumptuous repast."

"I'll see what he wants to do. He may be pretty busy, and if he is, he won't want to take much time for a meal."

"Well, play it by ear. We'll prepare food we can stretch or not as necessary," Molly said. "Just phone at the last minute, when you decide. You may, in fact, find he actually wants to talk to us…to find out what we know about all this." When she hung up, Molly felt almost giddy. Someone she knew and trusted was coming to help.

Anthony took over the phone, and Molly went to warn Ann about their coming need to share a bedroom. She found her with Georgia snuggled into a pile of pillows on Ann's bed, watching the small television Anthony had set up, with cable, for their entertainment. Helene had given them popcorn, which Molly shared as she filled them in on the latest developments.

Chapter 12

"I presume I will take over the orchestra for the rest of the year." Glen Quaverville was sitting across the desk from Anthony in his office.

"Don't presume anything, Glen." Anthony sighed wearily. "The committee is meeting this afternoon to decide if we should cancel the rest of the orchestra rehearsals and this weekend's concert."

"But…I'm the assistant conductor," Glen said angrily, standing up and leaning over the desk. "I'm supposed to be the one who takes over when the conductor's away."

"He's not 'away,' Glen. He's dead. There's a difference."

"I don't see the difference."

Anthony gave up in exasperation. "There's no more I can do for you now. Come by after the meeting's over, about four o'clock, and I'll tell you what we're going to do about the orchestra." He bent his head over his papers and began to work. Glen finally realized he was being dismissed and left the office, slamming the door behind him.

"I heard it all." Joey, the secretary, opened the door again. "Do you suppose that handsome young man thinks yelling and slamming doors will get him what he wants?" Anthony looked mournfully at her and nodded his head. She returned to her desk, leaving the door open as he preferred.

"Thank you, Joey. Thank heaven you're here," Anthony called after her.

His next guest was Agatha Holburn.

"A policewoman came and confiscated the scores and music we were using at the rehearsal last night. What are we supposed to do for tomorrow's rehearsal?"

"There may not be a rehearsal tomorrow, Agatha, so don't fret about the music now," Anthony said, not telling her the police had come to him first, and he'd had Joey show them to the library. "Call me after four o'clock, and I'll let you know what the department has decided to do about orchestra. Until then, nobody will be doing anything."

"All right, but they'd better not lose any of it. Some of that music is rented. I hope you have money in the budget to pay the fine to the publishers for all the parts we don't return on time if they don't get it back to us right away. And what are we supposed to use in the meantime? What could the police possibly want with it?"

"I have no idea, Agatha, but I'm sure there must be a good reason or they wouldn't go to all the trouble of picking it up," Anthony replied.

"It's your budget." She threw up her hands and left.

Anthony was surprised when Jolene appeared in his office half an hour later. He thought she'd be home or with family the day after her husband's death. But here she was, well dressed in designer jeans and matching jacket, a bright, patterned blouse with exotic jewelry setting off the outfit, and her long, reddish hair carefully done in a single braid. She'd never been a warm person, but he thought her marriage with Dr. Sneazewell had been as happy as was possible with such a man. In fact, he'd thought they were well suited to one another.

Jolene made it known, without hesitation, that she was there to remonstrate with Anthony about the removal of music from the library, especially the scores, which belonged not to the library, but to her husband. She wanted them back immediately. Anthony directed her to the police.

"I thought the least you could do would be to help a grieving widow," Jolene threw at him.

"I haven't noticed any obvious grieving," Anthony replied, "just a desire for some music scores. Why are you so anxious about those scores?"

"They were special to my husband, and I want to keep them in his memory."

"Well, Jolene, I'm sure they'll be looked after carefully by the police and still be a suitable memory when they get them back to you. Now, can I do anything to help with a memorial service for your husband, or is the dean helping you with that?"

"I hadn't thought about it yet, but I expect my father will help. More than you, at any rate. I shall tell him how unsupportive you've been." She flounced out of the office.

Anthony was getting a headache. He looked at the calendar and counted the months to the end of his term as chairman and the beginning of his sabbatical. If he survived the next eighteen months, he was sure he could survive anything. What a mess.

At one o'clock Andrew Penwith arrived and began his complaints. "I have just been accosted in the hallway by a Ruby I-don't-know-who violinist from the orchestra claiming I must have done something to Dr. Sneazewell because he died just after I talked to him at the rehearsal last night. I didn't even know the guy died, though I have to admit I won't miss him. Nor will anyone else I know." He leaned over Anthony's desk menacingly. "But where's she getting off at? I don't go for being attacked by hysterical women, and I sure didn't have anything to do with Sneazewell's death."

"Pay no attention to Ruby. The police are in charge of the investigation into Dr. Sneazewell's death. If anyone's going to make any serious accusation, it will be them. Just go about your classes and exams and leave the rest to the professionals."

"That woman belongs in a loony bin, anyway. She's really having a fit about the guy being dead. She acted like she was ready to beat on me, for Pete's sake. I know she was having it off with the guy, but what's that got to do with me, huh?"

"Ask Ruby. I don't know. Meanwhile, just tell the police anything you know about Dr. Sneazewell, and go back to your normal routine."

"Well, if you see her, tell her to lay off. I don't need hassle," Andrew said, and left the office.

As Anthony was gathering himself together after this last verbal attack, the phone rang. Joey answered the call and directed it to him.

After the call, Anthony went to the outer office where Joey sat at her computer.

"I was tempted to hide in the washroom until the meeting this afternoon, but instead I'm going to the hospital to see Trent Quillium. Apparently he's out of intensive care and asking to see me."

"That's good news, except why's he asking for you?"

"I don't know, but I'm off to find out. If any more members of the faculty or student body come by, please don't tell them where I am," he pleaded. "I'll be back in time for the meeting." He walked briskly out of the office, afraid he'd be waylaid before he could make his escape.

* * *

From the hospital's waiting room, Anthony phoned Molly, who had no classes for the day and was staying in Green Valley to shop for groceries and prepare the room for their latest guest.

After telling her what he was up to, Anthony asked, "Did you suggest to the police they take the music away from the library?"

"Mea culpa. Brian talked to his detective friend, Don—who happens to be in charge of the Sneazewell investigation—and told him to phone me. He's assured me there will be a thorough autopsy. I mentioned I thought Agatha and Jolene were in an awful hurry to get the scores out of the room, and maybe there was something in them they didn't want anyone to see. He listened to me only because Brian said I wasn't an airhead and could give him a lot of info on what's up in the music department. So I did. As I suspected, the officer hadn't passed on the information I gave him last night."

Anthony told her about all his visitors and then went down the hospital corridor to Trent's room. He was relieved Trent had survived the attack, but wished he found the boy more likable. Why did Trent ask to see him, in particular? Again he felt there was something familiar about Trent, something about the way he walked. He shook his head. He couldn't think what it could possibly be.

When he walked into the room and saw Trent lying in a web of tubes, looking small and pale and vulnerable, he wanted to turn and run...to get as far away as he could. It brought back the hours he'd spent at this same hospital watching Graham die only a year ago, unable to do anything for him. He didn't want to remember any of it.

Anthony forced himself to approach the bed and touch Trent's arm. The boy's eyes opened. When he saw Anthony, the ghost of a smile appeared on his face.

"Uncle Anthony," he said in a weak voice. "You came. I knew you would." His hand reached up to grasp Anthony's, and tears came to his eyes. He closed them and seemed to drift off again.

What was the boy talking about? Uncle Anthony? He didn't know what to say or do in response. Was Trent hallucinating? The hand holding his so tightly was warm and firm. He couldn't shake it loose and walk away. Overwhelmed by the boy's emotion, Anthony just stood there. He was looking around the room, trying to think what to do next, when he noticed one of Trent's feet sticking out from under the bedcovers.

He couldn't believe what he was seeing.

"The Clint toes," he gasped. Most people could move their big toe over the second one, but the Clints were born with the second toe on top of the big one. Could this boy be his sister's child? He pulled the covers gently over the boy's foot.

"Trent." He spoke the name quietly. The boy's eyes fluttered open. "What's your mother's name?"

"You know." Trent seemed to be half asleep as he spoke. "Regina Clint Quillium."

The tears sprang now to Anthony's eyes. His own kin, and he'd been treating him like a pesky fly, pushing him away every time he tried to get close.

"Why didn't you tell me before?" he asked.

"You didn't know?"

Anthony shook his head, unable to reply.

"I thought you knew. I thought you just didn't want me to let the others know, so they wouldn't start thinking you might play favorites. And then I thought you just didn't want me around, didn't like me." Trent's voice was a little stronger, and his eyes stayed open a little longer.

"I didn't even guess. I haven't seen or talked to your mother for over forty years. How is she?"

"But I thought you knew about that."

"Knew what, Trent?" Anthony could hardly breathe for the tightness in his chest.

"My parents died in a car crash last year. That's why I left the university."

At that point the nurse came in to give Trent a shot and suggested Anthony not stay much longer. When she left the room, Anthony told Trent he hadn't known.

"I thought it strange you didn't come to the funeral or speak to me about them," Trent said, and his eyes closed again.

As he sat watching the boy, who looked as if he had lapsed into a light sleep, Anthony marveled at the fact that this was his nephew, his family. It came to him how perilously close he had been to losing his only living relative. He began to feel very protective.

"Trent, what happened to you, the night you came to the church? Someone stuck a knife into you. That's why you're here. Do you know who did it?"

His voice woke Trent, whose eyes opened briefly. He began to speak slowly, breathily, though the medication was claiming him. "I remember setting out for the church to hear the concert. It was special. You'd planned Graham's dedication for me. I wanted to be there on time. Then my car ran out of gas." He rested for a minute.

"I remember leaving the car at the side of the road. I could run the rest of the way…get there on time. I didn't know of a gas station nearby." Trent's eyes focused briefly on Anthony, and he paused for a rest again. "And then…I heard a familiar voice calling me. I stopped. Looked around. There was a car. And then I felt pain, and I was falling. And all I could think of was getting to the church, everything would be okay there, and then…." Trent's eyes closed.

"Have you told the police?" Anthony tried to get a bit more from him.

The nurse returned just in time to hear the question. "They've been calling to see if he's able to talk yet. They said they'd be up this afternoon." She approached the bed. "And right now, I think our young man has had enough. I want you to go. He's not strong enough for long, emotional visits, but he was so anxious to speak with you, we let you in."

Anthony pleaded, "Could I stay just a few more minutes? I'll be careful not to excite him or tire him more."

Trent's eyes fluttered open briefly. He looked at Anthony and said, "We're all that's left, Uncle Anthony. Just you and me." He sounded content.

"I promise you we'll be family, Trent. As soon as you get out of the hospital, I'll take you home with me and we'll get you strong again."

Trent smiled and fell into a deeper sleep.

Chapter 13

"Let's go over it all together." Though nearly six feet tall, the balding Tucson detective, Don Jennings, looked short next to Brian Donegan. He'd decided to drive out to Green Valley when Brian passed on the invitation for supper. Perhaps Anthony and his friends would be able to give him more background on the people involved in his investigation.

Molly was so pleased to see Brian, she nearly hugged him. When he looked at her, his eyes hinted he might have been pleased if she had. The detectives, and what Anthony was beginning to call his harem, filled their plates with Ann's popular roast chicken, mashed potatoes, and gravy, and made the roomy kitchen table seem small. As they ate, Anthony told them all about his newly found nephew, and Trent's memory of a familiar voice calling to him from a car. Don had been up to the hospital to see him in the afternoon, but Trent hadn't remembered anything more than he'd told Anthony.

"Molly and I had a good chat on the phone this morning. She told me what's been going on." He turned to Helene. "Now let me tell you what I've discovered about your husband, Mrs. Hanson."

"Please don't call me that," Helene said in a disgusted voice. "I am Helene Benchwood, and I shudder when I hear that man's name. Just call me Helene."

"Right, Helene. Then you'll be relieved to hear that Edwin Hanson is in custody. His actions with your daughter are not his first attempts at sexual abuse. There are more serious charges against him. So far he's avoided being taken in, and we're glad to catch up with him. His bail has been set high enough that I doubt he'll be able to raise it. We don't want him to slip out of our hands this time. I think you and your daughter are free to return to a normal life, or as normal as it can be under the circumstances. We managed to trace Edwin's first wife and found out what he'd been up to."

"What was he doing there?" Helene asked, though she was already sure what the answer would be.

"His first wife threw him out when she discovered he was abusing their two daughters. She didn't press charges because she didn't want to traumatize her children even more. She just insisted he get out of town im-mediately, and as far away as possible. She thought it the best way to deal with him—he had to leave a good job without giving notice, which would make it difficult for him to get a job like it elsewhere. She told him she'd turn him over to the police if she ever saw him again, so he left town very quickly. Now he's wanted in several places. We haven't yet decided who's going to get him first."

"Let's just get rid of him. Let the East have him. The further away he is, the happier we'll be," Helene said vehemently.

"If only it were that easy," Don replied, "but we're working on it. Anyway, he shouldn't be a danger to you now."

"I'm so relieved. Now I can go out in public and hunt for a job so we don't have to scrounge off poor Anthony much longer."

"Helene, you and Georgia are welcome to live here forever, if you want. I love having a house full of people. It's so much better to come home to all this activity than to the emptiness of the last year. Don't even think about moving unless you don't want to stay. That's the only excuse I'll accept."

"Oh, Anthony, you are wonderful." Helene's eyes filled with tears, and she patted his hand. "Thanks for being our security blanket."

Georgia nestled closer to Ann, who she had made her adopted grandmother.

"Now it's time we had a chat about the music department," Don continued. "Brian and I need to know who's who there. All the victims are part of it, I understand, including you, Anthony. So, tell me everything you know about students, faculty, and friends who were around at each attack."

"I don't think we need to include Edwin in our considerations, Helene," Brian added. "From what you've told us, I don't think he suspected you were on to him when Anthony was attacked, so I don't think there's a motive there. The victims of violence have all been men. Edwin's specialty is preying on vulnerable female children."

They discussed all the musicians again, especially those present when Dr. Sneazewell died or just before—Glen Quaverville, Agatha Holburn, Ruby Reddick, Jolene Kaiser, who was Sneazewell's wife but went by her maiden name in the orchestra, and Andrew Penwith—and those at the church after Trent was attacked. Molly reminded them that Ruby, Andrew, and the unidentified man with the dark ponytail all came late to the concert. They speculated about the person who called out to Trent from the car. Since no one had mentioned seeing him walking to the concert that night, perhaps it had something to do with the attack.

"Did you know much about Dr. Sneazewell, Anthony?" Don asked their host. "We've looked him up, and traced his career and his wives. Jolene Kaiser is his third wife, and apparently she was an up-and-coming violinist when he met her at his last place."

"I didn't know about that," Anthony said. "I thought Jolene was his second wife, and I never bothered to find out who the first one was."

"A woman called Angela Handle preceded the present Mrs. Sneazewell. According to people who knew them, she was a promising violinist, too. Apparently this Sneazewell guy was a controller who preyed on these young violinists. They either fell for his charms or thought he could help their careers…or both. Instead, all he did was suck the confidence out of them and then dump them when they were completely demoralized. We traced Angela to a drug and alcohol rehabilitation place. She came out of there dry."

"Angela Handle," Molly said, "Agatha Holburn…it must be the same person. I always thought the name Agatha was too old-fashioned for her generation."

"Right. We've just put that together. Angela Handle/Agatha Holburn came back from her drug rehab cured, not only of her addictions, but apparently of Sneazewell, too."

"Are you looking for his first wife?" Helene asked.

"Yes. We understand she remarried. We're hoping to unearth some-one who knew him then and remembers her, and there will be marriage records where we can find her name. It just takes time," Don replied.

"Sneazewell may have been working on the next one or just having a piece on the side," Molly told them. "I've been told Ruby Reddick is his present fling; in fact, I've seen them going into a motel together. But she's in the second violin section, so may not be as tempting a conquest for what he considers marriage material. Not that there's any difference between first and second violinists."

"What do you mean?" Don asked. "Do they play the same instrument?"

"They're exactly the same," Molly explained. "They just play different parts in the ensemble or orchestra. However, violinists themselves, especially those who have played the first part, tend to believe they're more exalted than violinists playing the second part. Like prima donna sopranos who think second sopranos aren't quite so good as they are, because they sometimes sing the harmony part instead of always singing the highest, screechiest part."

"You're showing your prejudices, dear," Ann interjected as she continued knitting placidly. "Don't waste these men's time."

"I explained because these men, as you call them, are not musicians and may not get the significance of this first violin, second violin hang-up, Mother dear. Anyway, I've seen Ruby with another man, as well, though not close up. I don't know if he was a friend or something more. I feel very uncomfortable around her, and don't trust her, so I keep out of her way." She turned to Anthony. "I finally figured out she was at that meeting we went to. Do you remember?"

"Yes. I didn't want her to see me there. That's why we left early."

"What meeting was that?" Don asked.

"It's supposed to be an anonymous group."

"But it was an open meeting, Anthony."

"Anonymous. I am an alcoholic. Molly was at the open meeting as my guest, and Ruby was there speaking because it was her AA birthday, her first year of alcohol-free living."

"She couldn't have been Sneazewell's first wife, could she?" Molly began making connections. "That would be too much of a coincidence."

"We'll look into it," Don said.

"So we know Sneazewell went through women, though I can't imagine why anyone would fall for the guy," Anthony said.

"Apparently he could be very charming when he wanted to be. I spoke with someone who knew him 'back when,' and he told me Sneazewell used to charm the pants off most of the women he met, but he mostly enjoyed young violin students and went through them like a potter through clay."

"And then married the ones he wanted to destroy…or destroyed the ones he married, whichever came first. The two who are here are both musical has-beens. They play in the second violin section of the orchestra. They're past the age when they can make a concert career for themselves as violinists, and they seem to be rather bitter, as I would be if I'd had a potential career and been led off the rails. I wonder if Sneazewell drove all his women to addictions, or if he just married those who have the proclivity?" Molly said.

"Whatever he did, we'll be looking closely at the women in his life."

"Any news of Dr. Sneazewell's autopsy yet?" Ann asked, feeling she had been silent far too long.

"It will take a while. His neck was broken by the fall, but they're now checking for any drugs in his body, or a recent ingestion that could have caused the attack Glen Quaverville described."

"That's an interesting young man," Anthony said, and proceeded to tell the group about Glen's visit to his office. "A very ambitious man, and not afraid to show it. He's not very clever about the way he tries to get what he thinks he deserves."

"He had a package of tablets on his music stand. Sneazewell swiped them and put one in his mouth near the end of the rehearsal," Molly said. "The bass section is too far back from the podium for me to have seen the size or shape of the pill. Did you check with Glen Quaverville about it? Maybe someone gave it to Glen, and there was something nasty in it intended for him. And, of course, it's also possible Glen knew Sneazewell would borrow the package and take whatever was in it, and so put something nasty into it himself."

"Why would he do that?" Ann asked.

"He takes being concertmaster of the orchestra very seriously. I'm sure he wished Sneazewell would get sick and miss a rehearsal so he could take over and show the world how good he is," Molly told them.

"Maybe he just wanted to make the guy sick so he'd have a chance to conduct the orchestra, but went too far with whatever he put in the tablets," Helene suggested.

"But is he that ambitious?" Brian asked. "Would it be that important to take over an orchestra rehearsal?"

"Super ambitious," Helene said.

Don Jennings made a note of it. "What about the man who was talking to Sneazewell just before he had his attack?"

"Andrew Penwith," Molly replied. "He's young and has a giant ego. He thinks he should be in Richard Chamber's place as principal bass, and complains about being the fourth bass. He strikes me as just being a young pup who wants everything now...that is, right now. I suspect he was the hottest thing in his high school orchestra and finds it hard to accept there are others just as talented at the university level. He came in late to the chamber music concert. Then Trent came in, wounded, not too long after Andrew."

"That's interesting." Don made a note in his book. "Now, is it important what number player you are in a section? You said this Andrew was complaining about being 'fourth bass.'"

"It's the pecking order, and important to most people. Like managers and assistant managers and clerks in a store. The principal player gets to decide what bowings we use and how a passage is to be played, what style of bowing or phrasing to use. So the position should be given to the most experienced and competent player. Usually it is, but not always. There are politics everywhere, and seniority plays a part. Professionally, it's almost impossible to dump a principal player down the section. It's a huge loss of face," Molly explained. "And professionally, you get hired for extra jobs according to the number you are down from the principal."

"So it means a difference in the amount you get paid, and extra jobs for which you're hired, which ultimately matters a lot," Helene added.

"I see. Going back to the wives. The wives, you tell me, are now 'second violins.' So that's the equivalent of 'second class,' is it? Have they 'lost face,' too?"

"That's what first violinists think. And some are quite derisive about it. Someone who'd been a first fiddle and ended up near the back of the second fiddles would be devastated—upset and depressed," Helene offered.

"And very angry if they didn't think they belonged there," added Molly.

"This sounds as bad as police department politics," Brian commented.

"Every profession has its systematic pecking order," Molly said, and sighed. "It's so nice being past the age where I might have to care about any of that any more. I was never terrifically competitive, but the older I get, and the more liberated, the more compassion I feel for the struggling upwardly mobile. Poor lambs."

"I'm still competitive," Helene announced firmly, "but not enough to bump off those ahead of me in the section, or even the conductor, no matter how bad he is, for that matter."

They all laughed.

Brian turned to Anthony. "You must be pretty excited about Trent Quillium."

Anthony's eyes lit up. "That IS a revelation, the boy being my nephew. And the strange thing is, now I know we're related, I can see familiar traits. I'm quite excited about having family, though I'm sorry he lost his parents, and I'll never have a chance to know my sister. If only I'd realized there was a connection when he first came here, I might have met her before she died."

"Changing the subject, what have you been doing with the music you took from the library?" Molly asked Don. "Have you found anything in it?"

"No. But if they wanted to remove something, they had ample time. Still, I'm wondering why they want it back. Is there something in those pages they didn't have time to remove—something we haven't thought of yet?" Don wondered aloud. "The edges were quite soiled and felt a little greasy or oily. We're having an analysis done of some of them, though it's probably just sweat from the conductor's hands."

"Sneazewell had the nasty habit of licking his thumb or forefinger before he turned the pages of his score. It might have been oil from his fingers or bits of whatever he had to eat before the rehearsal that made them filthy. It was really disgusting," Helene told them.

"On the other hand, everyone in the orchestra knew he did that. They could use that knowledge if they wanted to get rid of him, like put some poison on the edges of the pages, knowing he'd eventually get to it," Molly speculated. "That could explain why Agatha and Jolene were in such a hurry to get the scores out of the auditorium, and their annoyance when they were collected by the police before they could remove the evidence. They probably took all the music so no one would wonder about missing scores. They probably thought everything would be safe from prying in the library."

"It's definitely odd they would be taking music to the library while their husband, ex and current, lay dead with a broken neck," Don said. "They could have been in shock, of course. Some people do very odd things when they're in shock."

"Well, they are an odd couple of women," Molly commented. "Trent Quillium used to hang around the library a lot. I wonder if he had anything to do with the music or saw anything unusual while he was there. Is he well enough to ask about his visits? He seemed pretty chummy with Agatha, although she paid no attention to him at orchestra rehearsals."

"When I saw him today, he was still very sleepy and on a lot of drippy things. I don't think he was in very good shape before he was knifed, so it might take him longer than someone who was healthy to start with. Some of these kids let themselves get too run down. Who knows when he'll be well enough to tell us more," Don said.

"Poor Trent. Bring him home to us, and we'll see he's looked after and fed properly," Ann suggested.

"I've told him he's coming home with me as soon as he's well enough to leave the hospital, and he seemed pretty happy about that," Anthony assured her.

"Couldn't we go to see him tonight? It's not too late. We could chat with him about his library visits, and maybe he might remember something helpful. Maybe he saw something unusual," Molly suggested. "Sometimes, after lying around all day, patients are wide awake in the evening and glad to be distracted by visitors."

"Good idea," Don said. "We'd better leave pretty soon if we're going."

Don phoned the hospital. He was told Trent was sitting up, and a short visit would be allowed.

They took two cars, Brian and Molly in one, Anthony and Don in the other, so Don wouldn't have to drive the others back to Green Valley after the hospital visit. Helene and Ann stayed home and sent Georgia off to phone her friends while the two adults cleared away the supper dishes. Georgia was delighted to be back in contact and eagerly anticipating her return to school.

As Helene and Ann loaded the dishwasher, they chatted about Helene's possible future. Ann wondered if Helene would have difficulty staying in the country.

"I'm a dual citizen," Helene assured her, "so it doesn't matter one way or the other, except for money. Instead of resigning, I took a leave of absence from my job in Edmonton. It was one of the few smart things I did when I married Edwin—instead of quitting my job there, I left my options open. I'll have to go back and see if I can shorten it. I may have to substitute teach somewhere till my leave is up. I don't have any money, but at least I don't have any debts, either. Edwin wanted to support us, so I just let him, not really expecting I'd have to think about going back to my job."

Chapter 14

It took the detectives and their passengers over half an hour to get to the hospital in Tucson. With Molly beside him, Brian enjoyed the drive. He always felt warm and comfortable when they were together. Don, in his car, found Anthony an entertaining passenger. Having had little previous contact with university professors or classical musicians, he enjoyed Anthony's stories about people in that world, some of whom Don had heard about vaguely and enjoyed learning more about.

When they arrived at the hospital, they went right up to Trent's ward. The nurse stopped them. "Trent's sister is with him now," she said. "I really don't think he should have this many more people visiting…where are you going?" she interrupted herself as the men began running toward Trent's room.

Molly alarmed the nurse further by grabbing her arm. "Trent doesn't have a sister. How long has the woman been here?"

"She just came. What's the problem? Why…."

They heard a shriek from Trent's room.

"Get someone in here who knows how to get Trent breathing again." Don and Brian met Molly and the nurse on their way into the room as they dragged a struggling red-haired woman out. The nurse called for emergency help and went to work on Trent, ordering Anthony to get out of her way. Don and Brian were none-too-gently pushing their captive ahead of them, away from the room.

"Who do you think you are?" she was yelling at them as she struggled. " I was just trying to help my brother."

"Help? Holding a pillow over his face?" Don replied, as he tried to pin her arms behind her back. "Molly, get hospital security up here now. And tell them to call for backup for me. Brian and I will get her downstairs and meet the officers there."

They propelled the surprisingly strong woman down the hall as she kicked and screamed, claiming she was being abused by the police. Molly didn't recognize the woman, whose smeared bright makeup made her look more like an old harridan than a relative anyone would care to admit to.

Meanwhile, the hospital staff had resuscitated Trent. Though even weaker than before, he was out of danger.

"No questions tonight," the resident told Don, who returned to the ward after handing his prisoner over to the backup crew. "This patient needs to be left alone."

"Can I just go in and let him know I'm nearby?" Anthony asked plaintively. "I'm his uncle—his only relative."

The resident looked at the detective for assurance Anthony was, indeed, a relative and an authorized visitor, and got his nod of approval.

"I'll be sending someone up to guard the room, Anthony," Don said.

"If they let me, I'm going to stay here with Trent overnight," Anthony told them. "I'm determined not to lose this member of my family now that I've found him."

As Don left to go to the police station to question the woman, he suggested Brian join him after taking Molly home.

* * *

On the way back to Green Valley on the freeway, Molly and Brian tried to figure out who the woman was, and why she was attacking Trent. Who did they not know about in this little drama? Was she the person who attacked him before, or the one who called to him from the car just before he was knifed?

The woman didn't remind Molly of anyone in the orchestra or the music department. She wished Helene had been with them. Having been there longer, she knew more people. She might have recognized who it was.

"I'm sure there's a library connection somewhere. It keeps popping into my head all the time. I've often seen Trent in there working with the librarian when I visit my bass locker just down the hall," Molly told Brian. "I've also seen Jolene in there a lot. Jolene must know Agatha was married to Sneazewell before her. I can't imagine how they managed to sit together in orchestra rehearsals all the time and still be not only civil to one another, but apparently close friends. As a matter of fact, I saw them look at each other in an almost conspiratorial way when Sneazewell fell off the stage. They weren't near enough to him to have done anything, but it seemed a little odd," Molly told Brian.

"Perhaps they knew what brought on the attack that sent him over the side, though. Maybe they had something to do with that," Brian replied.

"Frankly, it did look really fishy. I didn't say much to the officer at the time because he already thought I was just a silly old busybody. You know how so many of the youth think we're just old fogies, the geriatric set, the minute they see our graying hair," she reminded him, and added indignantly, "and this fellow so obviously thought I was gaga, I almost expected him to ask if I needed a good dose of Geritol to get me home."

Brian laughed. "Don't be neurotic about your age, Molly, just because you've hit the half century."

"I'm not sensitive about my age," she shot back. "I'm having a good time being in my fifties. I just resent being thought of as senile, or having Alzheimer's, or just plain a has-been."

"At least it's better than being thought of as a never-was, don't you think?" Brian said, laughing at her.

"Sometimes you youngsters make me very cross."

"Molly, it's great to be around you, if only to recapture my youth. However, I'm only five years younger than you, which doesn't quite put me in the youngster category. Actually, I'm the senior member of our department. My colleagues are already calling me 'the old man.'"

When they arrived at Anthony's in Green Valley, Helene met Molly at the door. "Dr. Gerhardt just called. He wants you to call him back as soon as you can."

"Who's that?" Brian asked Molly. "I don't remember you mentioning anyone with that name."

"He's my bass teacher," Molly explained. "He's a real sweetie pie, and I'm very fond of him. I learn a lot from him, even though he plays with a German bow. I don't know why he would be calling me. Did he say why? Isn't it a little late to call him back?" Molly's generation didn't make phone calls after ten o'clock in the evening. It was considered rude and intrusive.

"He didn't say what he wanted, but he did say it might be important. I don't think it's too late," Helene responded.

"These bass players, especially the ones with gigs at the clubs, are night hawks," she told Brian as Molly went to phone Dr. Gerhardt. "It was already after ten when he called, so he mustn't be playing tonight. I think he only does it a couple of nights a week, anyway, and mostly just jazz with his friends."

"What does Molly mean by 'even though he plays with a German bow'?" Brian asked Helene, while they waited for Molly to get through to Dr. Gerhardt.

"It's a bass bow with a wide frog on it. It's held in what I think is a peculiar way. Molly uses the French bow with a frog like that of a cellist, and she holds it the same as cellists do. The bows are quite different from one another," Helene explained.

"Frog?" Brian asked, new to all this music talk.

"That's what the part of the bow you hold in your hand is called. Come, and I'll show you on my viola bow." They went off to clear up Brian's confusion over the vocabulary. "We're not trying to be elitist, you know. Because we're so much with other musicians, we end up assuming everyone knows what we're talking about. It's just like in the computer world, or any other intense field, I suppose. I bet it's the same in the police world."

"You're right, it is," Brian replied.

* * *

Molly found Dr. Gerhardt's number where Helene had written it on the pad next to the phone. When he answered and they finished with the inevitable "how are you, fine, how are you, fine" ritual she hated, Dr. Gerhardt said, "I'm sure Dr. Clint told you we had a committee meeting today to decide what to do about orchestra for the rest of the term. He told us at the meeting about the other strange things that have been going on. We weren't aware of these until today. I was telling my wife about it tonight, and when I mentioned Sneazewell to her, repeating what Dr. Clint mentioned about his behavior just before he died, she was quite interested. I related to her your description of rehearsals, including Sneazewell's habit of licking his fingers before he turned the pages of his score, and she asked me if the man had any allergies. She's a family doctor and has patients with severe allergies—serious enough to require carrying around inhalants. That's a gizmo with something in it to keep them from dying if they're accidentally exposed to allergens. The substance causing the allergy is called an allergen. If they don't have the gizmo, they can die very quickly."

"I don't know that kind of detail about Sneazewell. They've confiscated the scores and are having them analyzed for poison."

"My wife says, if he had a severe allergy to anything, that would be a more certain death than most poisons. She says his behavior before he fell off the podium was consistent with a severe allergic reaction."

Molly could hear someone talking in the background.

"She just said to check for peanut allergies. Those are generally very serious. And some seafood allergies can cut breathing pretty fast. Bee stings can be deadly, too, but I doubt bees were buzzing around your rehearsal. It's worth checking for all those things, though. We all want to get to the bottom of this as quickly as possible. Dr. Clint said you know a detective, so I thought you would be the person to call about it."

"Thanks, Dr. Gerhardt. I'll get my friend Brian, from Edmonton, to pass it on to Don Jennings, the detective in Tucson who's in charge of the investigation. I now have a clear channel for passing on information, as the two are friends. I'm sure they can find out about allergies by asking Sneazewell's wife. She'd know."

"Well, I certainly hope this gets dealt with quickly. We're soon going to have to ask for danger pay to work in this department."

Molly related the conversation to Brian. "But, come to think of it, maybe with all his wives around, a wife wouldn't be the best person to ask, after all," she concluded.

"I don't recall Don mentioning an inhaler being among the objects in his pockets," Brian replied, "but I'll ask about that, and pass on the suggestions."

Ann joined them. "Where's Anthony? Has he gone to bed already? And how's young Trent?"

"I must get down to the station, Mrs. O'Connor," Brian said quickly. "Molly will fill you in on everything as soon as I'm gone." To Molly, he said, "I want you to be just as careful about doors. I'll phone as soon as I know anything, but don't expect me back tonight."

"None of us is going to be sleeping terribly well, so phone even if it's the middle of the night."

"I promise," Brian said.

Molly told Ann and Helene about the disaster they averted by their arrival at the hospital, then asked after Georgia.

"She's gone to bed. She wants to be ready for school in the morning, and I've promised to get her there one way or another. She can hardly wait to be back with her friends."

"I'll take her on my way to get Anthony from the hospital. He'll likely be a basket case by then. He's as old as I am, and we're not exactly fit for all-nighters."

"I'll go with you, and you can drop me off at the university. I have an exam tomorrow. I've had all this time to study, being cooped up here, so I'd like to go and get it over with," Helene said.

Molly looked at her in surprise. "Is that wise?"

"Edwin's the only one I'm afraid of," Helene said, "and he's in jail. I'm going." Helene had the set look on her face that Molly knew from experience meant she would hear no argument.

They finally went to bed after midnight, still hoping to hear from Brian.

Chapter 15

Brian hadn't phoned by morning, so the women proceeded with their plans. When Molly reached the hospital and got past the guard at Trent's door, Anthony was eager for information about the woman who attacked his nephew. Molly had to disappoint him; however, she told him about Dr. Gerhardt's suggestion as she ferried him home to shower and change before she took him to his office. He fell asleep in the middle of telling her how Trent's night had gone. From the nurse on the ward, Molly had already discovered he was recovering nicely, and the constable was there guarding the room, so she wasn't as worried about the boy as she was about Anthony. He needed his rest. She didn't disturb him until they got home.

An hour later they were driving to the university. Anthony had shaved and changed his clothes, but he still looked exhausted.

"Have you never regretted buying so far out of Tucson? Do you resent the long commute?" she asked him as they drove along.

He rallied a little. "Not when I can enjoy the mountains all around me. They're different every day. They change with the sun rising or setting, and the cloud formations are always amazing," he replied almost dreamily.

"You're quite poetic about it," Molly replied. "I see what you mean. Still, it's a long way, and I'd get tired of all the driving, I think."

"In eighteen months I won't have to drive," he said as he leaned back in his seat and closed his eyes. Molly let him sleep until they arrived at the music building.

"I'll pick you up shortly after noon, Anthony," she told him as he stumbled groggily out of the car. "I'm meeting Helene at my locker after her exam is finished, and then we'll come up to get you whether you're ready or not."

When Molly went to her locker well before noon to pick up some books, she heard loud voices coming from the direction of the music library, the sound echoing in the empty corridors.

"You stupid bitch. Can't the two of you do anything properly?"

Molly held her breath and backed into a crevice between two rows of lockers. She was wearing soft-soled shoes; obviously, no one had heard her in the corridor.

The strident voice continued in a threatening tone. "You really blew it."

Molly stayed where she was, straining her ears.

"What do you mean, blew it? None of us was near him when he died. I call that very good timing. It would have been better if you had made sure those scores were cleaned up before the cops took them. Where did anyone get the idea they were important, anyway? No one should even have noticed the music."

"Don't get in a snit. I'll bet that nosy bass player said something to them. I heard her saying the music shouldn't have been taken away. I doubt they even know why they came for the music, so keep your mouth shut."

"Cops," the first speaker said with contempt. "They'll probably look for some clues in the score, like loose paper or something. But they'll never find anything that could incriminate any of us. Just food on the paper. That's why it's so foolproof. If they analyze the page dirt, and I can't imagine why they would, they'll just assume it's stuff off his fingers or out of his mouth from something he ate, like a chocolate bar."

"All the little notes are out of the scores. The only other person who knows anything about those is Trent. And he's not doing much thinking these days. He was down here the day I was doctoring up the score. And the day Sneazewell complained about the notes."

"What else do you suppose Trent overheard, hanging around down here?"

"Nothing that matters."

"Well, who cares, anyway. We're dealing with him. But I am tired of being the only one around here who does any clear thinking. Just keep your cool till it all blows over."

Molly heard someone running down the stairs. This was one time when she hoped the hall was so dark no one would notice her cringing in her hiding place. She heard one of them say, "Someone's coming...I'm leaving." The library door slammed shut. She heard footsteps from that direction and held her breath again.

Molly recognized Helene's voice mumbling polite greetings to the person coming from the library. Then she heard someone running up the stairs. She peered around the corner and saw Helene nearly at the library door. She tiptoed back to the stairway and went to the top as quietly as she could, hoping she wouldn't meet whoever had just gone up before her. There, she turned around and came back down the stairs singing a theme from one of the Brahms symphonies in a loud voice to make her approach obvious. As she rounded the corner, she saw Helene standing by her locker.

"Hi, Helene, have you been waiting very long? I came as fast as I could," she said in her most carrying voice.

"No, I just got here myself," Helene replied.

"We're late picking up Anthony, so let's hurry." Molly wanted to get out of there as quickly as possible. "How was your exam?" she asked as they climbed the stairs.

"Just great," Helene replied, smiling, and the details kept them going until they were safely back up the stairs and in the corridor to Anthony's office.

Joey wasn't in the anteroom, and Molly sailed right through to Anthony's domain, nearly fainting with relief as she sank into one of the visitor chairs. Helene and Anthony eyed her with concern. She related all she could remember of the conversation she'd overheard from her hiding place outside the library, and they decided they should tell Brian and Don as soon as possible.

"Who passed you on the stairs, Helene?" Molly asked.

"Ruby Reddick."

"That's funny." Molly looked confused. "Why was Ruby Reddick in the library, I wonder, and who was with her? It didn't sound to me like the librarian, but I'm not all that familiar with their voices. It sounded as if she had some sort of conspiracy going with whoever else is still in there, but I could have sworn Ruby was the only one really grieving for Sneazewell. She seemed so grief-stricken when he died. Either that, or she's a darn good actress."

At that moment, Anthony's phone rang. It was Brian, asking if they'd seen Agatha Holburn or Ruby Reddick at the university that morning. Anthony repeated Molly's story. He could hear Brian conferring with Don in the background.

"We'd like all of you to stay together and wait for us there, please," Brian said.

* * *

Molly called Ann to let her know they'd be a little late. They had agreed to let each other know where they were all the time. Ann was alone at the house, and they didn't want her to worry.

Joey returned to the office briefly and asked if Anthony needed anything before she went out for lunch. When he said no, she closed his office door so no one would bother him. Most people knew he left the door open if he was free for visits. Shortly after Joey left, there was a knock on the door.

"Come in," Anthony said, wondering how Don and Brian had gotten there so rapidly.

The door was opened not by the detectives, but by Jolene. She closed the door carefully behind her. They were so startled by her entrance that none of them thought to greet her.

As usual, Jolene was elegantly dressed. Her long bulky jacket matched perfectly the color of her cotton pants, and her hair was drawn back in a very neat single braid. Only her eyes revealed something was terribly wrong with her. She put her hands in her pockets and stood looking around at the three of them.

"Good morning, Jolene." Anthony finally gathered himself together sufficiently to greet her, though apprehensively. "What can I do for you?"

Jolene ignored him and focused on the women. They sat stiffly, keeping their eyes on her, not trusting her.

Jolene finally spoke. "I thought I'd find you all here, gloating."

She had a wild, almost drugged look in her eyes. Her next remarks were directed to Molly. "You turned me in, didn't you?" She stared at her silently, waiting for a reply. Molly didn't reply.

Jolene's gaze moved from one to another. She couldn't help noticing their obvious fear. When she spoke again, her voice was contemptuous. "I'm not an addict like his other wives, you know. Not yet. And now, not ever. He'd like to have driven me to it, but I'm too strong for that."

As she pulled her right hand out of her pocket, she continued, firmly, "He didn't know how strong I was, and he didn't realize I'm always in control."

In her hand she had long scissors, held tightly, with the pointed end directed at Helene's chest. Helene looked even more terrified, and the other two sat frozen still.

"I saw the police car coming down my street this morning, so I just slipped out the back way and down the block to where I'd left my car. See, I thought ahead. They'll never know I've been to the library or here. Why would the grieving widow come to the university?" Jolene's slow smile was frightening.

The hand she drew out of the other pocket of her jacket held a long, double-edged knife. She pointed this at Molly's heart. "You didn't think I would notice you meddling in our affairs. Ever since you got here, you've been skulking around corners, with your 'sweet little old lady' sly way of pretending you're in another world while listening into conversations. I've been watching you for a long while." Jolene seemed relaxed and leaned against the door of the office. "So, big deal, you noticed us taking the music off the stands and didn't think we should take it to the library after the rehearsal. And I bet you're the one who told the police to take it away. No one else even noticed, much less cared…and wouldn't have, if you hadn't interfered."

With her last statement, Jolene gave a vicious thrust with the knife in her hand. It pricked through Molly's coat, but she managed to lean away from it and no blood was drawn.

"What are you talking about?" Anthony found his voice and tried to distract her.

"Shut up, you ineffectual old man." Jolene cut him off, her voice still controlled, though rage was on the edge of breaking through. Still, her hands remained steady as she held the knife and scissors dangerously close to the women. She didn't take her eyes off Molly or Helene, sitting side by side, and with each statement she moved the weapons closer to their hearts.

"When I leave this office, you'll all be dead, and poor little Agatha will be found in her corner in the music library, having committed suicide with these same instruments, unable to live with what she did." She looked at them all, one by one, and then laughed.

When they didn't react, she went on. "And I am free of that man, and will be free of all of you. Say your prayers."

Suddenly the office door against which Jolene had been leaning burst open, knocking her off balance. Helene and Molly reached up in time to deflect the weapons pointed at them. Brian came through the door.

"Grab her," Anthony yelled, almost leaping over his desk to help.

Brian was not alone, and in the ensuing scuffle Jolene was disarmed, handcuffed, and led away by the officers. She had become very quiet but continued to dart venomous looks back at her three victims.

Anthony gave Brian a shortened version of the confrontation while Helene and Molly got their equilibrium back. Then they all quickly trooped downstairs to the music library. They found Agatha, as yet uninjured, sorting music. Don asked her to accompany him to help with the investigation into Sneazewell's death. She left with him, looking confused, asking how she could possibly be of any help. After locking the library, the others went back upstairs to Anthony's office.

"I need a drink," Anthony said.

"No you don't," Helene and Molly replied in unison, though at that moment they could have used one themselves.

Molly turned to Brian. "I know you'll want to quiz us, but first we need to hear from you. Give," she said, plunking herself down in a chair different from the one she'd been in when Jolene entered the office. "Everything since we saw you last." She gave him her best schoolteacher look that said he'd be sorry if he didn't do as he was told.

"When I got back to the station," Brian began, "Trent's assailant had been fingerprinted. The prints matched some the computer bank had on file for a Dick Jensen, recently released from jail after having served time for violence. His wig fell off when he scuffled with the officers again, so they weren't surprised she was a he. Although he has a very pretty face, they thought he was too strong to be female, and that was confirmed when they searched him at the station. Anyway, Don started on him, laying charges for the two assaults on Trent. When Sneazewell's murder was added to the list, Dick became much more cooperative. Attempted murder doesn't carry as big a stick as a successful murder."

Brian paused. "Could we be allowed to have some lunch during all this?" he asked pitifully. "It's a long story. I'm hungry, thirsty, and tired, and I want to get back to join Don."

Molly got up quickly. "I'm sorry, Brian. How selfish we've been. Of course you're tired. You've been up all night. We should have gone right home, anyway, where you could get some rest."

"I told Don that's where we'd be." Anthony got up to lead the way. "Where's your car, Brian?"

"Outside this building. I got an official sticker from Don."

"We'll come in for it later. None of us wants to miss any of your story, so it will be better if we drive together," Molly said.

"The car shouldn't be left there, Molly. You drive Brian," said Anthony.

"You shouldn't be driving, either." Molly looked with sympathy at the two men, noticing the dark shadows under their eyes.

Brian stopped the procession.

"Listen, I'm going to join Don," he said. "I want to be in on the questioning. I'll grab a bite to eat on the way there. I promise I'll tell all when I get home. I shouldn't be too long."

They couldn't persuade him to go home with them and rest, so they parted ways, their curiosity unsatisfied.

Chapter 16

It wasn't until much later they heard the story from Brian, having had to be patient until he returned to Green Valley and had a good night's sleep.

After they fed him a mammoth breakfast and served him his second cup of coffee, they demanded to be told all. He leaned back in his chair and surveyed the people sitting around the table in this warm, comfortable kitchen—Molly and the friends he'd made in the short time he'd been there. He looked longest at Molly, who always seemed to have people around, always involved with so many. His heart tightened. He wanted to become more than one of this woman's friends. But it was too soon after the death of her husband to even approach her. It would have to be enough just to see her occasionally. He would be patient, but he had hopes.

"We finally got the whole plan out of Dick Jensen, Ruby's husband. Yes, she'd married again after Sneazewell. Ruby and Agatha confirmed much of Dick's version. Jolene was either blabbing almost incoherently, giving us more detail than we wanted or needed, or sitting in sullen silence. Dean Kaiser has been down, demanding she be allowed to go to her shrink and telling them she's too sick to be in jail. I feel sorry for the old geezer. He brought her a lawyer, but she wouldn't stop talking even when he told her to.

"Anyway, for you it all began when the three wives of Sneazewell ended up in the second violin section of this orchestra. I won't bore you now with the long story of how that came about. Nevertheless, the upshot of it is, Sneazewell was getting a big kick out of it, deliberately seating

Jolene and Agatha together. At first, he probably didn't think Jolene would realize his first two wives were right there, still under his direction, still in his control through the orchestra. When he engineered an affair with his first wife, he must have been having a ball. Ruby tells us he was absolutely triumphant. This was the ultimate domination. He didn't know he was signing his own death warrant and he probably never suspected the slaves would ultimately revolt. Ruby tells us she was using him. I'm not sure who was using who the most, but there they were.

"Anyway, the women found out how they were all connected to each other through Sneazewell, but didn't let on to him that they knew. They got together and decided to get rid of him. They all had different agendas.

"Agatha thought they were going to get rid of him by scaring him away. Hence the notes, which they all helped to write.

"Ruby got money out of him, but she hasn't told us yet how she managed that. She's a plotter, though, and had a lot of time to build up her hate. Ruby is also a great little actress, so it's hard to know when she's telling the truth and when she's just setting the scene for what she wants you to believe.

"Jolene, on the other hand, planned all along to get rid of him permanently, and was just using the two ex-wives. She considered them gullible and weak. She was livid when she first discovered Sneazewell was making fun of her by flaunting his former wives in the orchestra. She hadn't been with him long enough for her self-esteem to be totally destroyed, so she still had some fight. However, she also has a history of being a little unbalanced. Sneazewell likely didn't know, or he might have been more careful with her, I suspect. Jolene married him while she was away studying, and her father could never decide how much to tell the new husband about her medical history. When he met Sneazewell, he didn't like him much and just didn't tell him anything. When Sneazewell applied to this university, the dean thought that if the man was working here, he could at least make sure his little girl was all right. He didn't know anything about Sneazewell's ex-wives being here, or how Sneazewell was trying to destroy Jolene, but he still felt the need to have her close by.

"Jolene was the one who knew how serious Sneazewell's peanut allergy was. The others hadn't done any research on it, but she had. They just accepted what she told them—an allergic reaction would frighten him because he wouldn't know what brought it on. It would make him vulnerable like they all were.

"So Dr. Gerhardt's phone call was a help. His wife will be glad to hear that," Molly said.

"Yes. Thank her for the suggestion," Brian replied, and continued.

"Ruby wasn't completely free of her addictions yet, but was trying, through AA. Or at least she pretended to be. This is still being investigated. A drug connection here is still being looked into. Sneazewell may have been using. We'll know with the autopsy. Anyway, Ruby's new husband, Dick Jensen, was using her to deliver drugs through her AA meetings. They both claim she didn't know what was in the packages she delivered to his friends. As I said, though, she's a good little actress, and it's hard to know whether to believe anything coming out of her mouth. She'd have to be really stupid not to know what she was carrying, and stupid, she isn't. She'll be dealt with separately.

"Dick Jensen also pretended to be an artist to explain their income. He claims Sneazewell blackmailed Ruby into sleeping with him again. That's what Ruby must have told him. Hence, you saw them going into a motel, and so did Trent. Sneazewell loved baiting his wives and probably made sure Jolene 'accidentally' found out about the motels. This, of course, only made her more determined to get rid of him. She wasn't a woman to trifle with.

"Agatha, still a psychological mess, was financially dependent on the pittance their divorce agreement required him to give her for a period of time. He used the requirement to keep her tied to him. He was a master puppeteer, with Agatha very much an emotionally battered wife. Although she'd kicked the alcohol and drugs, she was still often severely depressed and insecure. She was weak enough to follow whatever plan the other two wives suggested, thinking they were her friends. None of them ever expected to be found out. They thought the stuff on the score was a foolproof plan, because it wasn't a poison. Who would ever expect a music score to be a weapon?

"Jolene was the ringleader—the planner—and she's proud of it. In her own unbalanced way, she's the strongest of the three. Sneazewell apparently never told anyone he had this severe allergy. He didn't want anyone to think he wasn't always in full control. He certainly couldn't have known Jolene knew about it, or he might have been more careful. I got the impression, from her babbling, she was present when he accidentally ate something with peanuts in it and had to use his epipen. He probably wouldn't expect her to notice anything like that."

"What's an epipen?" Georgia asked.

"It's like an epidermic needle. People who have severe asthma or allergies carry one with them all the time. It's filled with epinephrine, or adrenalin. He needed to inject himself immediately if he came in contact with peanuts. Jolene saw, didn't let on, read up on allergies, and realized she had the perfect weapon. The investigators found a book on allergies hidden in one of her drawers at their home.

"So, they set out to frighten him, to make him feel vulnerable. They wanted him to know what it was like. They wrote the poems to put in his score to make him think someone was after him, to get him on edge. They were very annoyed when it didn't seem to work. He just became angry with Agatha, suspecting her because she always picked up his music so was the only other one who had access to it. This guy was such a power nut he wouldn't even carry his own music, for heaven's sake. He loved having his minion keep the scores in the library and ordering her to bring them to his office whenever he wanted them. From Jolene's perspective, of course, this was a perfect setup.

"Anyway, they decided to apply peanut oil to the pages of one of his scores, so when he licked his fingers and turned the page, he'd get just a little bit into his system. That would give him an allergic attack. He wouldn't know why. It would be mild but recurring, and he'd get frightened. They'd be laughing every time it happened.

"At least, that's how Agatha and Ruby saw it. Jolene intended to make sure he didn't have his epipen with him and that the dose on the score he'd be using would be sufficient to do him in.

"Then Trent interfered. None of them had any use for him, but they could see he was curious about them. He'd seen Ruby with her 'nail polish' working on a score when she was in the office one day, and they were afraid some day he might make the connection if the police found out about the peanut oil on the pages. He was asking too many questions.

"They followed him the night he was attacked, hoping to catch him alone. Things worked out perfectly for them when he ran out of gas and tried to get to the concert on foot. It was dusk, and they were able to get his attention. When he stopped to try to see who was calling to him, Dick was supposed to injure him just enough to keep him out of their way for awhile. Dick went too far—he has a tendency to violence—and Trent was nearly out of their hair permanently.

"This upset Agatha, but Jolene knew if Trent was alive, he was still a danger to them. She began making plans to have Dick Jensen finish the boy off, especially after Sneazewell reacted as she had planned he should and died as a result of their 'prank.' Jolene was able to keep the other two quiet because they were part of the conspiracy, though Agatha and Ruby hadn't intended it to go as far as it had.

"Jolene convinced Dick he had to kill Trent or he'd go to jail for the first attempt. She thought it would be easy for Trent's 'sister' to visit him at the hospital, so Dick got all dressed up, and off he went. He's not terrifically bright.

"Then both Ruby and Jolene began to worry about Agatha. She might go to the police to tell what they'd been doing to Sneazewell—all the poems they'd put in his scores, trying to scare him, and the stuff on the score. She was the weak link. She was already very upset about Sneazewell dying, even though she hated him. She didn't have Ruby and Jolene's ability to shake off the ultimate result of their actions. They couldn't afford to let her loose in case she ended up feeling she had to tell the police what they'd been doing. That's why she was Jolene's next intended victim."

As they were refilling coffee cups, Ann suddenly said, "None of what you've said explains who attacked Anthony, or why."

"Trent and I had a long talk in the hospital," Anthony said. "When I was sitting with him after his attack, he kept saying, 'I didn't know you'd hurt yourself, I didn't mean it to happen.' Apparently, he came to my place to get the family connection out in the open, but in my drunken state I didn't give him a chance to speak, told him to go away, and climbed out of the pool to throw him out. He left in a hurry, and didn't realize I'd hit my head as I dived back into the pool. Of course, everyone in the music department knew about my injury by the time I got back to work, what with the bandages decorating my head. I just told people I'd lost my step getting out of the pool. I would have drowned if our friend from Mexico hadn't hauled me out."

"And who trashed our house?"

"We don't know," Brian said. "It happened the same night Georgia and Helene left home and you three were at the concert. If Edwin was able by some devious means to find out where Molly lived, it could have been him looking for Helene and Georgia. If so, he didn't find any evidence of them here. Maybe it was Edwin on the phone trying to terrorize Molly, figuring she'd know where they were and maybe would let something slip out about their whereabouts. That's the only thing I can think of. Incidentally, the phone call to Molly's home in Edmonton was probably from Edwin. It would be one way he could get Anthony's unlisted number—or maybe one of the faculty members at the university gave Edwin Anthony's address."

"Well, let's just rejoice that neither Anthony nor Trent died, and that Edwin is locked away where he can't do any more damage for a while, anyway. I hope none of those women will be back at the university to harass us, though I do feel sorry for Agatha." Molly got up to get the coffeepot.

"But that's your thing, Molly," Helene said, knowing her all too well. "You're always having to feel sorry for someone."

Chapter 17

Trent's doctor decreed that he was well enough to be sent home. Anthony picked up his nephew at the hospital and drove carefully out to Green Valley. His precious cargo enjoyed the colors of the world, so startling and such a joy to someone who has been in the bleak surroundings of a hospital for any length of time. Helene and Georgia had collected his belongings from the barren room he rented near campus, and his car had been retrieved from the area where he'd left it the night he was stabbed. There hadn't been much to pack at Trent's place, where his belongings, all suffering from neglect, were carelessly strewn around the room.

Trent looked a little shaggy, though the beard he'd grown in the hospital suited him. Anthony decided to stop at the barbershop he had visited regularly for years and get his nephew tidied up so he'd be presentable to the group awaiting him at his new home.

It was a transformation. With his now neatly shaped beard and mustache, and the well cut hair, Trent looked like a very respectable young man who could be taken for any of the rising young executives in the city. Anthony was surprised at the radical change, which also revealed more of the family resemblance between them.

When they arrived, no one was visible in the house. Anthony took Trent to the room they'd fixed up for him, where he was greeted by a big computer-generated sign, saying, "WELCOME HOME, TRENT." Gathered in the room were all the current residents of Anthony's house. His new extended family echoed the greeting.

Trent's throat seemed to close. He was sure if he said anything he'd burst into tears.

Though Ann had never met him, she was comfortable assuming the role of everyone's grandmother. She stepped over to Trent, gave him a gentle hug, and whispered into his ear, "It's okay to cry, Trent. Manly men do cry." Then she stepped away and said aloud, "Georgia's the sign maker."

Trent looked around the room and saw there were tears in everyone's eyes. Even the detective fellow, who had come down from Edmonton, had moist eyes. Trent had been taught to believe his easily shed tears were just another sign of his being a wimp, but these people he barely knew and that beautiful girl, Georgia, were all acting as if it was okay.

He let the tears come.

When they'd finished their orgy of hugging, crying, and laughing at each other, Trent was exhausted. Ann insisted he lie down on his new bed to rest while lunch was being prepared, and he did gladly. Ann tucked an afghan around him, fussing and clucking over him like a mother hen, and then they were all gone, leaving him to drift blissfully off into a euphoric sleep, snug in all the love and attention he was getting.

An hour later, when Trent awoke, Anthony was sitting at the side of the bed looking down at him.

"You're looking so much better, Trent. I'm much relieved. Ann asked me to see if you're ready for some lunch."

"Thanks, Uncle Anthony." Trent suddenly felt ravenous. "I'm starved," he admitted.

"Ann will be glad. She thinks you're looking peaked and we need to fatten you up. She also doesn't think your wardrobe is adequate, and we should go for a shopping trip as soon as you're well enough."

"I don't want to disappoint Ann," Trent said, looking worried. "But, I really can't afford to do that. We didn't have much money, and by the time I'd paid the funeral bills and debts when Mom and Dad died, there was just enough left of the insurance for my tuition and a little for living expenses if I'm very careful. My clothes will be fine when I wash them up."

"Ann and Georgia have already done that, and she's still insisting. And I would be delighted if you would let me look after your expenses. I have no children. I've missed that pleasure. I'd like to look after you as if you were my son, instead of my nephew."

During Anthony's speech, Trent's throat was closing again, and he could feel the tears returning. His uncle was going to think he did nothing but cry. He couldn't speak.

"Then it's settled. You save what's left of your inheritance for spending money, or what you'll need when you graduate and are looking for work."

"Uncle Anthony, that's more than generous. After the way the rest of the family talked about you, I can't believe you're being so kind to me. My grandparents and parents didn't want me to take up music," he confessed, turning his head on the pillow away from Anthony. "They said it corrupted you, and I would end up to be just as decadent as you are. They didn't want anything to do with music. They thought it ruined you."

He turned back to look at his uncle. "I wanted desperately to play the cello. I don't know why, I just did. They finally relented, but they didn't like to hear me practice, and they didn't like to see me with it. They never came to my concerts. Even when I won scholarships, they acted as if it was a bad thing. Nothing I did ever pleased them, and I worked so hard to be so good they'd have to like me."

"You are an excellent musician, Trent," Anthony assured him, "and you're also a very good human being."

"They wanted me to go to Rice University because it was close to home, and they thought I should take something 'useful' instead of music," Trent continued. "But I wrote around to all the universities in the states nearby, sending in audition tapes, and when you answered from the music department here offering me a playing scholarship, I recognized the name, Clint, and wondered if you were my uncle. I was curious about you. That and the scholarship, of course, is why I came here to study. Mom and Dad were angry when I chose to go so far from home, and I've had to work very hard to stay. I didn't see much of them after that, and when they died in the car accident, I felt terrible, as if I'd abandoned them. See, as their only child, I was such a disappointment to them. I couldn't ever make them happy."

"I'm sorry they felt like that, Trent. But, if my opinion counts, I think many people would be very proud to have you as their son, and I'm sure your parents loved you very much. They may not have been able to show it. Your grandparents weren't very demonstrative. And maybe they poisoned your parents against me so much, they suspected every musical son would 'go wrong.' Your mother was a lot younger than I, and they had many years to turn her against me. They must have preached their own disappointment and hatred for what I was," Anthony suggested.

"But why did they hate you so much when they didn't even know you anymore?" Trent asked.

"That's what prejudice does. Even when I was growing up, having a gay child was shameful, and the child a sinner, so your mom was probably taught to believe I was not someone you should be allowed to resemble in any way. Your grandparents didn't believe I was born the way I was, so they blamed it on music. They thought I wasn't 'manly' enough because I wasn't playing rough sports and taking out girls, so something must be wrong with me. It was less painful for them to think it was all the fault of music rather than accept a child of theirs might be just plain born that way. And in those days, people loved to blame the parents for anything going wrong in a kid's life, and they were all afraid of what the neighbors would say."

"It's such a waste," Trent said, in a tired voice.

Anthony got up, "Listen, fella, I thought you said you were hungry, and Ann is going to be very annoyed if I don't bring you to the kitchen so she can start fattening you up. Let's leave the heavy stuff, and get busy making you healthy again."

* * *

It was Brian's last day in Arizona, his plane leaving Tucson at four o'clock, and he and Molly were off to meet Don Jennings for lunch. Brian wasn't really looking forward to leaving, but he'd promised to spend Christmas with his sisters and their families in Edmonton. The children always looked forward to their uncle's company, and the presents he showered on them because he had no children of his own.

Brian and Molly had spent the previous day Christmas shopping for their respective families and friends. Molly's son, Patrick, was spending Christmas with his grandparents and was apparently still enamored of the girlfriend who didn't impress Molly. Shannon and Erin, her daughters, were flying into Tucson the next day. Thank heavens Martha was looking after the house. Brian was taking packages back for Martha's brood and Patrick and his grandparents, as well as what he'd picked out for his nieces and nephews.

As they drove along to meet Don at the restaurant, Molly said, "I'm going to miss you, Brian. You've been such a good friend to us all."

"I'm sorry to leave, too, but you'll be surrounded with so many people you won't even notice I've gone," Brian replied.

"I'll notice," Molly said, quietly.

Brian briefly took his eyes off the road to look at her. "Will you really?" he asked.

She looked at him, and he saw something in her eyes he hadn't seen before. "Yes, Brian. I don't always think of you as our friendly problem solver. I really do like you for yourself, not just as a detective."

"That's important to me, Molly." Brian now kept his eyes on the road, wishing he didn't have to drive at all, but not daring to stop the car and push the moment.

"I think of you a lot, Molly. On the one hand I wish you would keep out of trouble—so you'd be safe. But on the other hand, I want to see you again, and I'm afraid if you're not in trouble, I won't be invited back into your life."

"I won't have to be in trouble just to want to see you again, you big goof. I enjoy your company. I want to see you again. Whenever you have time to travel. Or when I'm back in Edmonton," Molly assured him. "We're good friends now, aren't we?"

"I am eventually going to want us to be more than that, Molly." Brian paused, and then took a deep breath, deciding he had to say it. "I love you. Ever since I met you in the library that first time, I've wished I had someone like you to spend my life with. I've not said that to another woman since my wife and I split. And that's a long time ago."

Molly's heart seemed to swell up into her throat. "No," she said, needing to stop his speech. "It's too soon to talk that way. It would be disloyal to Paul for me to even think about caring for someone else now."

They were silent for a while. Then Brian tried again. "I've always thought the biggest compliment a woman who'd had a good marriage could pay to the man she'd loved all that time was to want to marry again," he said in a quiet voice. "I know you and Paul had a good marriage. I saw you together. You liked each other as well as whatever else you felt for one another. You were having fun." He paused, and sighed. "I was jealous."

They were both silent for some time. Then Molly responded.

"Can we just be good friends for awhile, Brian? I have to get my world sorted out before I can commit to anything. I care about you already. But I can't think of you as anything but a good friend until I've finished burying Paul. He's still in my head and part of my very being, and I suspect always will be. I can't just chuck him away."

"I wouldn't ever want you to 'chuck him away,' as you put it. He was too decent a man. I've had only a small taste of life around you, though, and you seem to surround yourself with good people. And lots of them." Brian laughed suddenly, a happy sound. "I love your mother and the way she still treats you, at fifty, like a little kid. And the banter you have. And your closeness to Anthony, and Helene, and all their attachments. You have good friends. If all I can be is a friend for now, I'll accept being part of that circle."

They had arrived at the restaurant Don claimed served the best Mexican food in Tucson—Brian's favorite food. Not seeing Don's car there yet, they lingered for a moment before going in.

Molly finally leaned over and kissed Brian on the cheek. "I really am very fond of you. And I will miss you when you go home. Of course you're part of what you call my circle. You're one of my favorite friends, a valued friend." She opened the door and got out. Brian followed her into the restaurant, understanding the subject was closed for now.

While they were waiting for Don Jennings to arrive, they talked about Anthony's household.

"I hope Helene and Georgia accept Anthony's offer for them to stay for the rest of the university year. She loves her courses and playing, and Georgia seems to have made a lot of good friends down here," Molly said.

"Did you know Anthony has asked Helene to marry him, and live with him there?" Brian asked.

"Anthony? Marry a woman? You ARE kidding." Molly laughed.

"Molly, don't be so naive. Gay men often marry, or have purely platonic arrangements with women, just to placate the people around them. As a front. I'm surprised he didn't do it early on, when his parents were so upset with him. Many live that way, with compliant women, and seem perfectly happy to do so."

"She didn't tell me about the offer. Is she going to accept?"

"She was asking my advice, actually. I'm the outsider down here, so a little easier to talk to about it. She was so disappointed in her first marriage and then her pseudo marriage to Edwin, she can't see ever wanting to marry for romantic reasons again. I suggested if that's really the case, she should go ahead. She could do a whole lot worse than marrying Anthony. They get along well together, and with Anthony at least she won't have to worry about her daughter being attacked by the man in the house."

"That alone would almost make it worth doing," Molly agreed. "I think I'd kill the bastard who ever tried it on one of my daughters," she said vehemently. "I was ready to kill Edwin myself."

"I'm glad you didn't get to him before we did," Brian replied. "I'd hate to have to visit you in jail. Have you decided whether or not you're going to stay here for the next term?"

"Now that Anthony has a houseful, I know he's not going to be lonely, so I'm not needed. But I haven't decided what I need yet. I'm still recovering from the first term. I don't have the energy to think about the future."

"If you decide to stay, can I come to visit all of you again?" Brian asked, looking at her in a way that confirmed feelings he had expressed in the car.

"You'll always be welcome. I'm sure we'll all be glad to see you," Molly replied. She just wasn't ready to answer the look in his eyes. She hadn't had enough time to grieve properly for her husband. She didn't want to become involved with a man just because she depended on him. She never wanted to depend on anyone. Yet she found herself incapable of being totally aloof, of keeping a distance. She didn't want to hurt him, and didn't want to lock him out of her heart.

"But let's just be good friends for now," she said again.

She hadn't closed the door on him. She'd just postponed the opening.